Al[f]

'"Get out! . . . I'll murder the rotten lot of you."

There was a moment of silence. Then they came out in a rush, skipping and laughing and cracking their tails like whips, six of them – six big rats.

Batty, the oldest, lay on his back and rubbed his stomach. "We're rotten now. Rotten rats – that's what we are."

And then they meet Alf . . .

MICHAEL GRATER

Alf Gorilla

Illustrated by the author

A Magnet Book

First published 1986 by Lutterworth Press
This Magnet edition published 1988
by Methuen Children's Books Ltd
A Division of OPG Services Limited
Michelin House, 81 Fulham Road, London SW3 6RB
Copyright © 1986 Michael Grater
Printed in Great Britain by
Cox & Wyman Ltd, Reading

ISBN 0 416 06432 9

This paperback is sold subject to the condition
that it shall not, by way of trade or otherwise,
be lent, re-sold, hired out or otherwise circulated
without the publisher's prior consent in any form
of binding or cover other than that in which
it is published and without a similar condition
including this condition being imposed
on the subsequent purchaser.

for the staff of the zoo who would never have let it happen

or would they?

Alf Gorilla

from the museum

from the zoo

Chelsea

Battersea Park

Clapham Junction

Lavender Hill

Soho

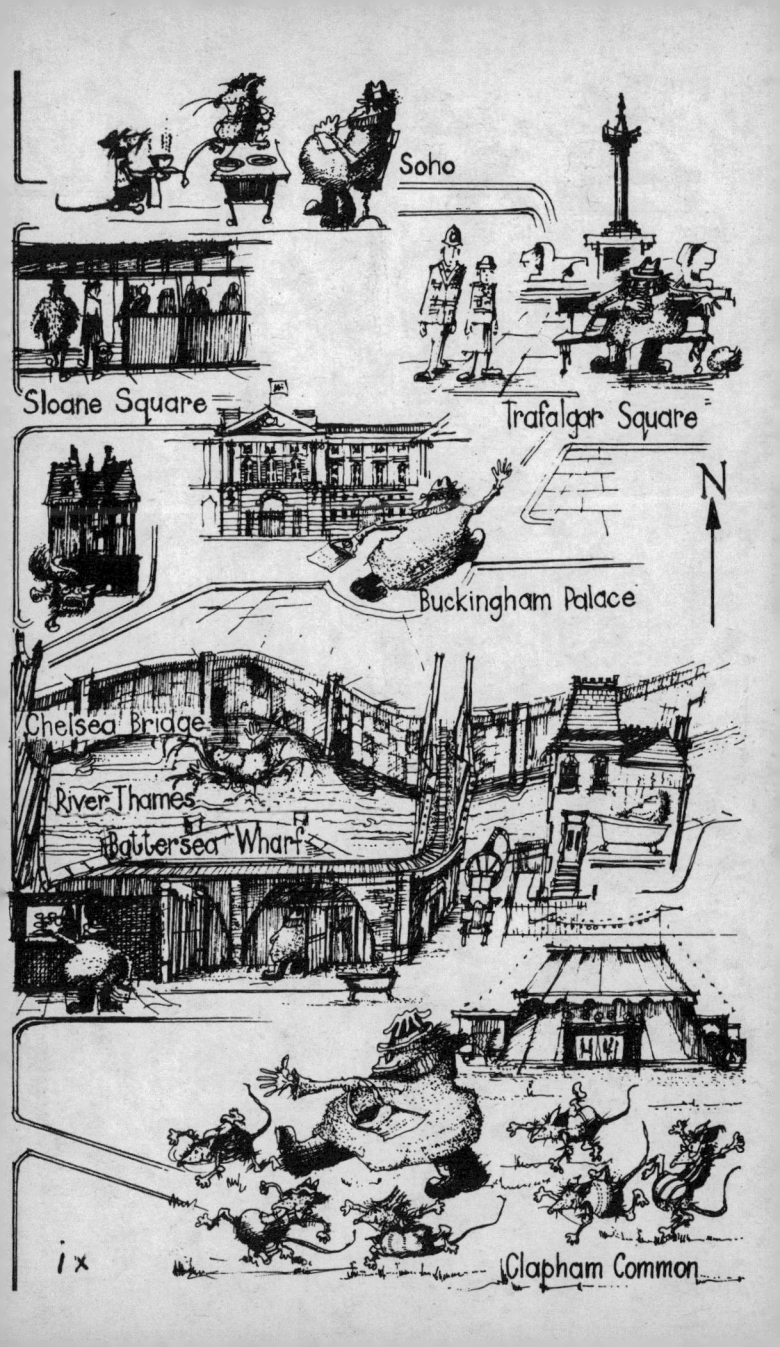

Sloane Square

Trafalgar Square

Buckingham Palace

N

Chelsea Bridge

River Thames

Battersea Wharf

Clapham Common

Chapter One

"Get out!" Bennett stamped round his store, kicked his barrow and splintered a box. "I know you're here – pinching the fruit. I'll murder the rotten lot of you."

"Get out!" Crash . . .

"Get out!" Crash . . .

"Get out!"

Suddenly he was quiet and they knew he was out of breath and changing his coat ready to go home. They stayed still until they heard him slam the door and walk along the cobbles past the other arches. There was a moment of silence. Then they came out in a rush, skipping and laughing and cracking their tails like whips, six of them – six big rats.

Batty, the oldest, lay on his back and rubbed his stomach. "We're rotten now. Rotten rats – that's what we are."

"And you're the rottenest." Sid, his second-in-command, had a hat made from a foil pie-case. He crushed it tighter between his ears.

"Not me, Sid."

"You're the boss."

"Right!" Batty wore a hat cut from a sock. He kept it on all the time because he could think better when his head was warm. "Check 'em then," he said. "Make sure they're all here. We've got a busy night."

"Quiet!" Sid stood on his hind legs and shouted. It was an order. He called the roll.

"Clappy?"

Clappy, from up the road at Clapham, was hanging by his tail from the lamp.

"Ready for tonight?" Sid asked.

"Is it on then?" Clappy twisted in mid-air and landed on his feet.

"Looks like it. You ready, Orse?"

Orse, short for Australia where he came from, was sorting out tangerines. "I'm ready, Sid."

"Weston?"

"Hold on, Sid. I've fallen through the lining."

Bennett's working coat, hanging where he left it, was wriggling.

"Weston!"

"Sorry, Sid . . ." The voice was muffled. "I dropped my glasses."

"Weston . . . we're waiting!"

Weston's nose poked out of the pocket, twitching.

"You ready?" Sid spoke sharply.

"I will be, Sid." Weston put on the glasses. They were important because he was the official rat-reader.

"Totters? Where are you?"

A marrow began to edge slowly across the floor.

"Totters . . ." Sid jumped at the marrow and kicked it. "Get out from under there."

Totters did a back somersault and ducked a second kick.

"You ready?"

Totters shrugged.

"All present, Batty."

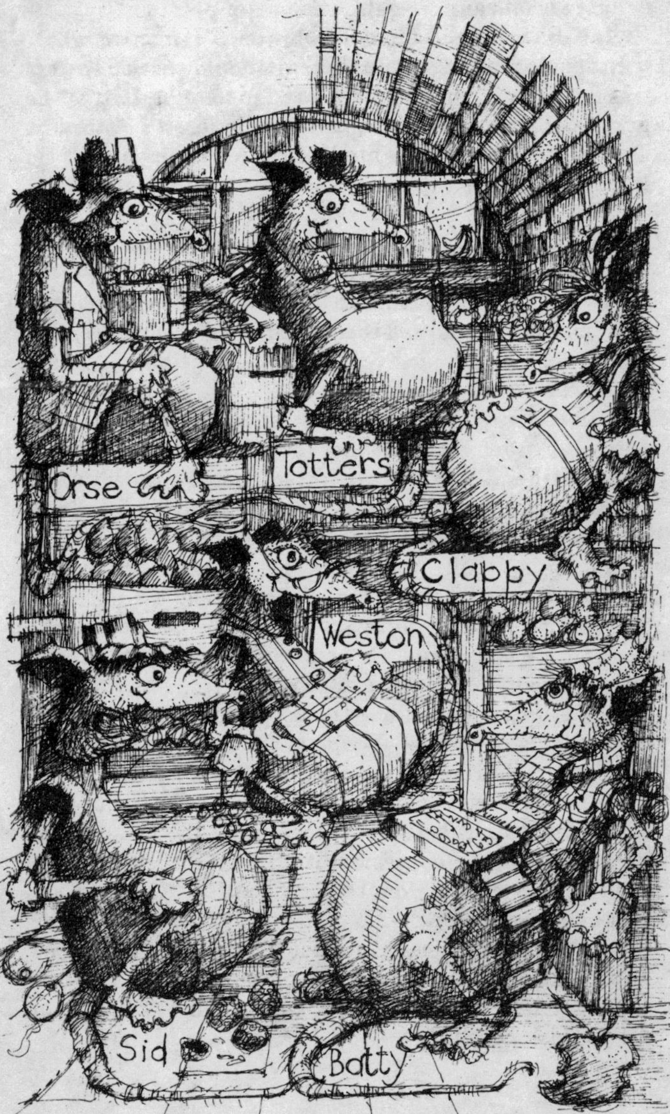
Orse
Totters
Clappy
Weston
Sid
Batty

Batty was leaning against a sack of potatoes.

"Is it on then?" Sid wiped his whiskers. "Is it on tonight?"

Batty looked serious but before he could answer Totters was in front of him. "Do we have to go tonight, Batty?" he asked. "It's our night for a salt-beef dinner. It's Saturday. There'll be a lot of people about. It could be dangerous." He looked round for support.

"Tonight!" Sid flicked his tail but Totters just managed to duck again. "It's tonight if Batty says so." He turned to the older rat. "Is it really on?"

Batty placed his thumbs in his braces which were made of rubber-bands knotted together. He pulled and let them snap back on his jersey. "Tonight . . ." Snap . . . "It's tonight."

"But it's Saturday," Totters complained. "We could do it one day next week. It's not urgent."

"Not urgent! Not urgent, Totters! Look!" Batty tugged the scarf away from his neck. "Nearly strangled me, didn't he? Look at the marks."

"Go on . . . look." Sid pushed the younger rat.

"That's right. Take a look." Batty held up his chin. "Look where he had me by the throat. The hair's all gone . . . and it's still sore." He stroked the bare patch. "It'll happen again . . . tonight or tomorrow . . . could be any one of us. When Oily Sludge comes at you out of the dark, Totters, you'll know it. You won't want his claws round your neck. He's got to be stopped . . . once and for all."

It was a serious moment, broken only when Orse cracked a walnut between his teeth. He lifted the floppy brim of his hat. "I appreciate it's urgent," he said, "but I ain't sure we should do it tonight, Batty. There's a moon. It'll be like daylight."

Batty nodded. "That's good. It'll help the Big One. We don't know if he can see in the dark, and we don't want him fumbling about blind, or getting lost. Everything ready this end, Sid?"

"All ready, Batty. We've made it comfortable for him – and private."

Batty carefully put his scarf back on. "Tonight then."

"What about dinner?"

"Forget it, Totters." Sid stepped between him and Batty. "We'll take our own rations. We'll stock up before we go. And we'll need bananas – lots of 'em."

Batty knew Sid could be trusted with the details now that he had made the decision.

"Right." Sid understood. "We'll start with the route." He helped Weston spread out a map of the London Underground.

"First . . ." Weston cleared his throat. "First we cross the river the usual way. Then we go straight up there." He pointed.

"What's that?" asked Clappy.

"That's Pimlico station – on the blue line. We're going by Underground because it's quicker. We catch a train there – three stops to Oxford Circus. Then we change to the brown line – one stop after that and we're there."

"Got it?" Sid asked. "We'll split up for travelling and meet when we get there, under the last seat on the platform. And take care. It'll be dangerous. OK, Batty, we're ready."

Batty looked at the watch which he wore round his middle like a boxer's prize-belt. Weston was teaching him to tell the time. "It's five to eight . . ." He twisted the watch round. "Or five past. We must be there and away by midnight – with the job done. Let's go."

Sid snapped out orders. They helped themselves to Bennett's fruit, waited just inside the door for the whistle, then followed in single file out to the wharf.

OPERATION MINDER had started.

Chapter Two

The journey went as planned. They crossed the river by the railway bridge and then went fast but carefully through the back streets to the Underground.

They separated at the station because it was well lit and busy. A single rat, or even two, could slip by unnoticed but a bunch of six travelling together was likely to cause a fuss.

As the train stopped, Batty and Sid scrambled onto the roof and were followed by Clappy and Orse, but Weston and Totters thought it undignified to ride outside when they were passengers. Totters slipped into a shopping basket and was carried into the train, while Weston used the fur-coat trick. He picked out a passenger with one almost touching the ground, and as the crowd pressed towards the doors he slipped inside the coat and hung comfortable and warm in the lining, with his tail out of sight.

"How was it?" Totters asked when they met again.

Weston smiled. "Warm – and the coat smelt a lot better than Bennett's. How was the basket?"

"Rode on her lap and she didn't know, did she?" Totters gave him a friendly punch.

They met the others and did a single-file exit from the station, with Clappy and Orse scouting ahead. This was a tricky bit, Sid reminded them. If they were careless they could be in serious trouble. There were vultures there, and giant owls who could see in the dark even better than rats. They had to stay close together or else . . .

The Big One was pretending to be asleep when they arrived. His hands were folded on his stomach, but although he seemed relaxed on his straw bed his eyes were not completely closed. He had seen these night visitors before. Now they were back – more of them this time. He waited with a smile just touching his lips.

"Smashing . . . just what we need," Weston whispered. "Look at the size of him. Look at his chest. And his hands – they're bigger than we are."

"I bet he eats a lot," said Orse.

"About the same as Bennett probably," Batty answered. "But we've got plenty of food for him. Watch him now. He knows me and Sid. He's used to us." Batty stretched to his full height and took a step towards the cage. "You awake?" he whispered.

The gorilla opened the eye nearest to him. It glowed red in the light which was left on at night.

"It's Batty. I said we'd be back. Remember?"

The gorilla opened the other eye.

"Banana . . . Totters." Sid pushed him towards the cage. "Give him one through the bars. We always start with bananas."

"You sure he understands?" asked Weston.

"Certain. Batty's talked to him a lot. Go on, Totters. Don't be scared. Give it to him."

Totters held out a banana.

"Closer . . . he's not dangerous." He gave him another push.

The gorilla stretched out an arm and took the banana delicately. It surprised Totters who expected him to grab it. When he took the first bite they saw his teeth.

"Look at his choppers," Orse whistled softly, "like a man-eating shark."

"Just right for Oily Sludge." Sid stood close to Batty. "Go on," he said, "tell him. He understands you. Tell him while he's in a good mood. Tell him it's tonight."

Batty gave the gorilla a smile. "It's like I promised.

Tonight. We're taking you out. Everything's ready."

The gorilla was on his second banana. He slapped his stomach as though he needed to help the first one down. It boomed like a drum.

"Shshshsh . . ." Batty looked round in alarm. "You have to be quiet. Don't make a sound. Just do what we tell you." He turned to Sid. "Get the door open."

"Clappy . . . Orse . . ." Sid pointed to the bolts.

"You can come out now." Batty put his nose through the bars. "I said you can come out."

The gorilla sat still.

"He's not exactly keen, is he?" said Orse.

"Because the door's still shut." Sid checked the bolts. "We'll open it for him."

The door was heavy but they worked on it. They pulled with their arms and legs and even used their tails. They pulled together, but it stayed shut.

The gorilla watched smiling.

"Pull . . ."

"It's no good pulling." Sid unhooked his tail. "It must open the other way. We've got to push."

Batty looked anxiously at his watch. "Hurry up . . . do it together. Push . . ."

Nothing.

The gorilla shuffled towards them.

"You push it," Batty encouraged him. "You're strong. It's too heavy for us."

The gorilla leaned on the door, but it stayed shut.

"Pull it then. Go on, pull it." They made anxious signs to him. He hooked his fingers in the bars and leaned backwards. The door still stayed shut.

"Now what do we do?" They looked at Batty.

The gorilla solved the problem. He put a single finger, black and wrinkled, against one of the bars and slid the door sideways. As the gap opened he leaned through and grinned.

"It's a sliding door – like the Underground. He knew all the time." Weston spoke for all of them. "We should have thought of that. Not stupid, is he?"

Batty looked at his watch again. They were behind schedule. "You can come out." He beckoned. "It's safe. Just step down here with us."

The gorilla eased himself through the door and climbed down to their level, where he stood with his knuckles on the floor supporting his weight.

"He seems friendly," said Weston hopefully.

They dressed him in the keepers' room. The brown overall coat was a tight fit, and Weston was worried about the length of hairy arm sticking out of the sleeve. But it had to do. The cap was slightly better. Weston tipped it over the gorilla's eyes so that the peak hid the top part of his face.

The gumboots were a problem. "He's got such big feet,"

Weston complained, "about two sizes bigger than the keeper." But the gorilla helped by tucking in his toes and pushing hard. They wrapped a scarf round his neck to cover his chin.

It was time to go. Batty looked at his watch, then took it from his waist and held it out. "For you," he said, pointing to the hairy wrist. "It's a present from all of us – a welcome present."

The gorilla liked it.

"Fetch the broom, Totters."

They showed the gorilla how to hold the keeper's broom with the bristles touching the ground. When Batty stepped back and half closed his eyes he might have been looking at one of the keepers. He nodded, satisfied. It was time to take their minder to a safe place – to take him home.

Chapter Three

The walk through the streets was the gorilla's first test. The problem was to know how he would behave once he was out of the zoo.

Batty travelled with him, tucked down inside the scarf, with Weston on the other side giving directions. The others went on ahead. To be safe Weston made the gorilla walk in the darkest shadows, and when possible they used the back streets. He walked well. He seemed confident with his new friends in his scarf, and seemed able to sense danger.

When they saw a policeman ahead they managed to turn him in his tracks and make a detour round the block. A bit later, when they came across a group of people taking up most of the pavement, he stepped into the road and tried to use the broom as they passed. It was as though he understood.

When they finally arrived at the railway arches Sid and Clappy were ready with the gate open and had the gorilla inside before Batty and Weston were out of the scarf.

As they walked along the wharf to the arch where

Bennett stored his barrow and fruit the gorilla's nostrils quivered and he smacked his lips. He had got the scent of the celery Bennett left soaking in a bath outside.

Batty winced as he saw his watch go under the water, but it was in a good cause. "Eat as much as you like," he said bravely. "Help yourself. Put both hands in." The gorilla did.

"Bennett's going to be mad on Monday morning,' said Clappy. "There won't be any left if he goes on crunching it up like that."

"He's mad every morning." Weston was more worried about the mess the gorilla was making down his coat. He whispered to Batty. "If I'm going to keep him well dressed we'll have to teach him to eat properly. Gorillas have got terrible manners."

When the celery was finished the gorilla took a drink from the bath. He made loud slurping noises which they enjoyed, and when they laughed he made them even louder.

"Everything ready inside, Orse?" asked Batty.

"Perfect – comfortable and warm, just like you said."

"Plenty of fruit?"

"The best."

Batty looked at the river and up at the sky. It was beginning to get light. "Inside then." He flicked his tail towards the arches. "Get him out of sight."

Orse whistled to attract the gorilla's attention. He had a banana in each paw.

"Don't give him them till he's inside," said Batty. But he need not have worried. The gorilla was already following Orse into the arch. It was one of a row under the railway, and had a door set in the wooden partition which filled the side. When the gorilla went through the door they followed and pulled it shut. Orse handed him the bananas.

"Now we have to start teaching him." Batty placed himself in front of the gorilla and looked up, serious but

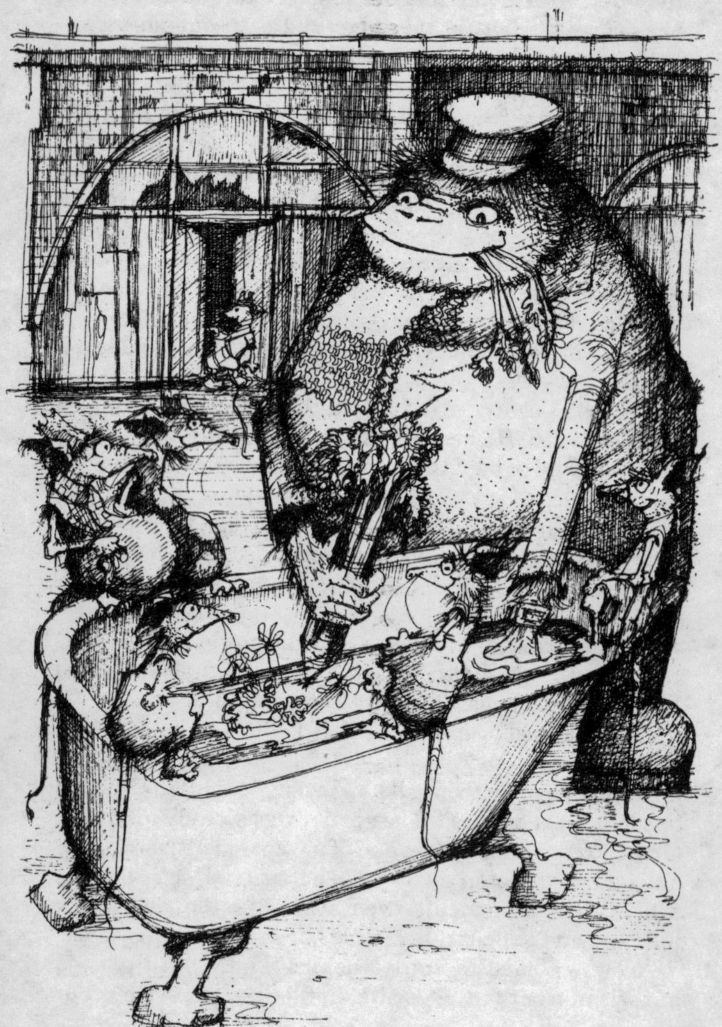

smiling. "Listen carefully. This is where you're going to live now. You'll like it here. Orse . . . this is Orse . . . is housekeeper. He's got it ready for you. It's comfortable – more like a hotel than a cage. But you have to do what we say. Understand?"

The gorilla dropped the banana skins on the floor.

"We'll have to teach him to be tidy." Orse carefully picked them up. "You mustn't leave evidence lying about, Sport. This place is secret. Nobody knows you're here."

They were in a space just inside the door. It seemed impossible to go in any further because the arch was piled high with old furniture.

"This is a barricade to stop anyone else coming in," Orse explained. "We've built it special. But there's a secret way in. You can get through when you know how. Just follow me. Do what I do, and stay close or you might get stuck." He led the way. "Under the table here . . . past the coal scuttle." He dropped the banana skins into the scuttle. "Inside this cupboard . . . then out through the back. Now we turn and go along this tunnel."

At the end of the tunnel he pointed upwards. "We have to climb here." He jumped onto a chest which had the drawers open to form steps. The gorilla followed easily. They climbed until they came to a gap at the top.

"Mind you don't fall. It's a trap, a sort of moat like you get round a castle. We cross it here. Jump . . ."

They jumped.

"Now if you lie on your back you should just have room to wriggle under the top of the arch. Then roll over . . . like this."

Orse rolled over and dropped out of sight. The gorilla followed. There were mattresses spread on the floor to catch him, and, as he bounced, Orse scrambled out of his way. The others followed. They were all laughing.

"This is it. It's your new home." Orse spread out his arms. "All yours."

It was a bigger space than his cage – and different. The

floor was soft, with a carpet stretched from the mattresses to the wall. There was a bed, a table and a tall armchair – and on the table a bowl of fruit.

"This is your bed. You sleep on this now – not on straw." Orse patted the pillow.

The gorilla went straight to the table and lifted himself up. He settled on a corner and helped himself to the fruit.

"You're not supposed to sit there." Orse sprang from the bed to the armchair. "You're supposed to sit here." He jumped up and down on the seat. "It's a chair. It's very comfortable. Look – it's got springs."

The gorilla climbed down from the table and into the chair and began bouncing like Orse. It creaked under his weight.

"Not too much or you'll break it. When you sit in a chair you keep your feet on the floor – not on the seat."

"And you take off your hat and coat when you're indoors." Weston pointed to a coat-stand. "You hang them up like the ones already there. They're for you. They're your best clothes." He turned to Batty. "Are you sure we can make him human?"

"Not at once," Batty said. "Although he's big, bigger even than Bennett, he's a child really. We'll have to teach him everything. It's all new to him – except for the fruit, of course."

When it was time for bed they got his coat off and the boots, but he would not let them take the cap.

"It makes him feel important, Weston. Let him keep it on." Batty smoothed the covers over the gorilla's stomach.

When he seemed to be asleep the Battersea gang tip-toed away and huddled together on the mattresses. They made their usual tight group, a mixture of ears and tails, close together, relaxed but ready for any emergency. They were tired but they had done it. They had a minder, and the worst danger was over. Now they could catch up on some sleep.

Chapter Four

The outside gate creaked.

"Bennett!" Sid hissed. "Bennett's here."

The rats recognised the sounds: the noisy gate, the boots on the cobbles, Bennett's door scraping.

"Thieves! Robbers! It's the celery now, is it? As well as the fruit."

Batty and Sid turned to the sleeping gorilla.

"We must tell him . . ."

"Make sure he doesn't panic . . ."

"Keep him calm . . ."

"I'll murder the rotten lot of you – I swear I will."

Sid jumped onto the bed and crouched by the gorilla's ear. "You awake?"

A hairy hand reached up and pushed the cap back. The eyes were open. The face, right by Sid's nose, was black and wrinkled. Sid was glad to feel Batty at his side. "Listen . . ." he spoke quietly. He pointed to the wall. "That noise next door. Don't take any notice. It's nothing. It's only Bennett. He's noisy and very rude, but he's harmless."

"I'll stretch your skins on the wall . . . with nails."

Batty smiled. "He doesn't mean it. He shouts at us every day."

"But you have to understand," Sid whispered. "Bennett mustn't know you're here . . . ever. So when you hear him, don't take any notice. You'll get used to him."

"I'll poison you . . ."

"He doesn't mean it. He's a sort of friend." Batty watched the gorilla carefully. He seemed to understand.

The shouting went on until Bennett was ready for market. As soon as they heard him drag his barrow out their own day started.

Clappy and Orse went up the wall and through loose bricks into the next arch. They had to get the gorilla's breakfast.

Weston, the gorilla's personal valet, laid out the clothes for the day. There was a dark overcoat and a black hat which Weston had borrowed from an office in Westminster.

After breakfast they put a bowl of water with soap and a scrubbing brush on the table. Gorillas, they guessed, do not wash themselves. So they did it for him. He liked the taste of the soap, and as fast as they put it on he stretched out his tongue and licked it off.

They put on the new overcoat and the scarf and helped him with his boots, but he was not sure about the hat. In the end they had to persuade him that the cap was only for sleeping in, to keep the light out of his eyes. The other hat made him look very special.

"Human!" Batty whispered the word, hardly believing what he saw.

"Shall we let him look?" Weston was pleased with the change. "He won't recognise himself." He pulled open the wardrobe door so that the gorilla could see himself in the mirror. "What the well-dressed gorilla looks like," he said proudly.

"The well-dressed human," Batty corrected him. "Remember, he's human now."

The gorilla looked at himself from every angle.

"Specs!" Weston suddenly remembered. He scrambled onto the gorilla's shoulders and placed a pair of sunglasses gently on the black nose. "I hope he can keep them on," he said doubtfully.

"Ready?" asked Batty.

Weston nodded.

"First lesson then, Sid."

Sid snapped out orders, forming them into a line with the gorilla in the middle. "Now!" He held the end of a length of string, and as he spoke he gave it a tug. An old toy cat, black and very battered, jumped out of the back of the wardrobe.

"Cat! Cat!" They shouted together as Sid dragged it in front of them.

"Cat! Cat!" They jumped about and made faces and lashed out with their tails.

"Again!" Sid pulled the cat the other way.

"Cat! Cat!"

"And again!"

They practised until the gorilla joined in. "Come on . . ." they shouted. "It's a cat! Cat! Cat!"

He could not shout but he looked fierce and growled and showed his teeth, and beat his chest.

Batty nodded to Sid. It was what he wanted.

After the cat lesson they showed the gorilla how he should walk without leaning on his knuckles. He seemed to find it difficult to stay upright because his stomach was full and heavy at the front. But Batty, whose own stomach was large enough, showed him how it helped to lean backwards when he walked.

They kept at it all day, improving him all the time. Batty watched closely. If the lessons went well he had promised the gang an evening out, to make up for their lost Saturday.

* * *

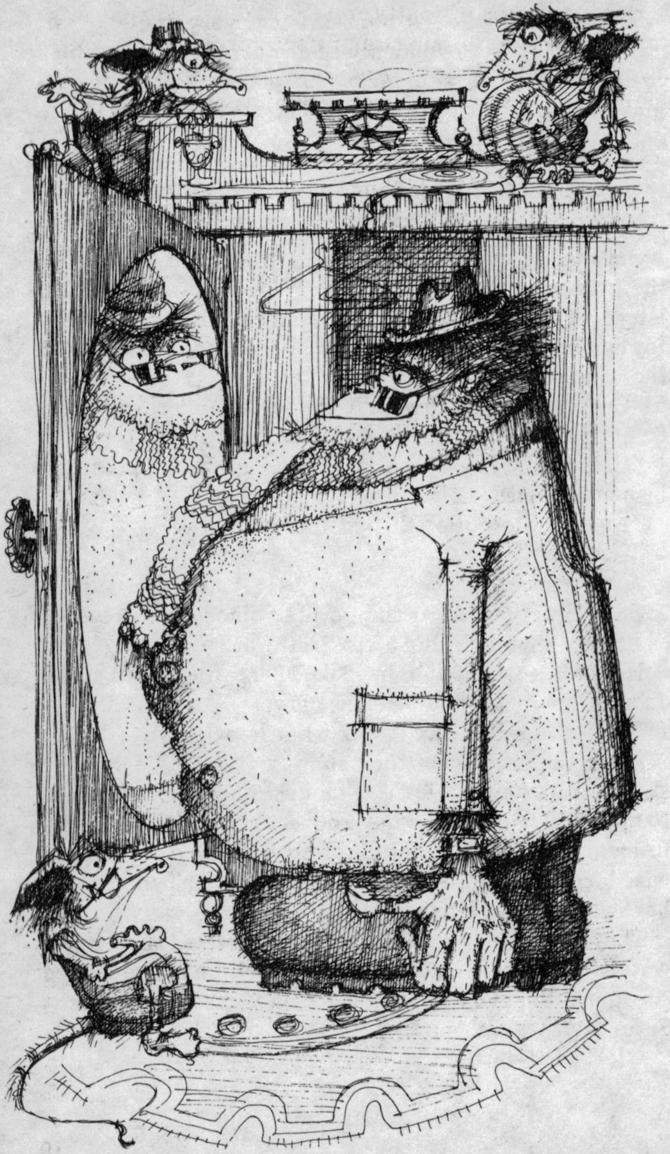

"I think he's ready, Batty, really ready." Weston was walking backwards, encouraging the gorilla. "He's walking upright now . . . look. And the glasses are staying on. The disguise is perfect. We can take him out tonight, can't we?"

"You've done a good job . . . all of you. Perhaps we can try him." Batty placed himself where he could look directly up at the gorilla. "Smashing . . . you look great . . . really human."

The gorilla looked down and nodded.

"Really human and important. If you behave yourself . . . if you remember what we've taught you, we'll take you out. You'd like that, wouldn't you?"

The gorilla turned and looked at himself in the mirror. He liked what he saw, and smiled. He was ready.

Chapter Five

Cats are a problem to rats and there are some bad ones in Battersea. But Oily Sludge was probably the worst of the lot. The gang called him Oily because he could slide under almost anything, and they called him Sludge because he was the same colour as the mud on the wharf at low tide – grey streaked with black.

They hated him because he lived on their patch and was getting vicious. He had even taken to lying in wait for them. It was his recent attack, when he had caught Batty by the throat, which had decided them. Now, thanks to Operation Minder, he was going to get what he deserved.

Oily Sludge had a voice as rusty as the corrugated iron shed he lived in. As they crept closer they could hear him croaking to himself.

"Delicious. . ."

They had timed it well. They knew he would be home in the early evening. It was why they were calling on him first.

"Delicious . . ." It sounded like a blunt saw ripping through wood.

They edged closer.

Oily Sludge had a delicatessen chicken between his paws. He had shoplifted it earlier in the evening, and was licking the fat on the outside. He was not really hungry. He rarely was. He was too good a thief for that. But a cooked chicken was a good way to start the night.

The jelly and fat melted on his tongue, and made the tip of his tail twitch with pleasure. At that moment, just as he was about to take another lick, there was a tap on the door. His ears pricked up. He had not heard anyone coming.

There was a second tap, timid – as though the caller was afraid to disturb him. He slid the chicken silently to one side.

Tap . . . Tap . . .

He frowned. He rarely had visitors. The shed was his special private place. He stretched his well-sharpened claws.

Two taps again, slightly more urgent.

He rose without a sound. The door was hanging loose on its hinges, with a gap at the bottom. He took a step towards it – and another, pausing to listen before he put his head through. He used what was left of his whiskers to feel the way, slowly – very slowly.

It was already dark outside and the air was cold on his nose. He crouched low and inched forward. That was his mistake. He should have come out in a rush.

"Cat!"

The rats shrieked and hurled themselves against the door, trapping him by the neck.

"Cat! Cat! Cat!"

It was a terrible shock for Oily Sludge. One moment he was ready to pounce, and the next he was trapped by the neck, and even worse – face to face with something he could not understand. He was not a coward. His eyes were sharp and he had recognised his old enemy, Batty. But

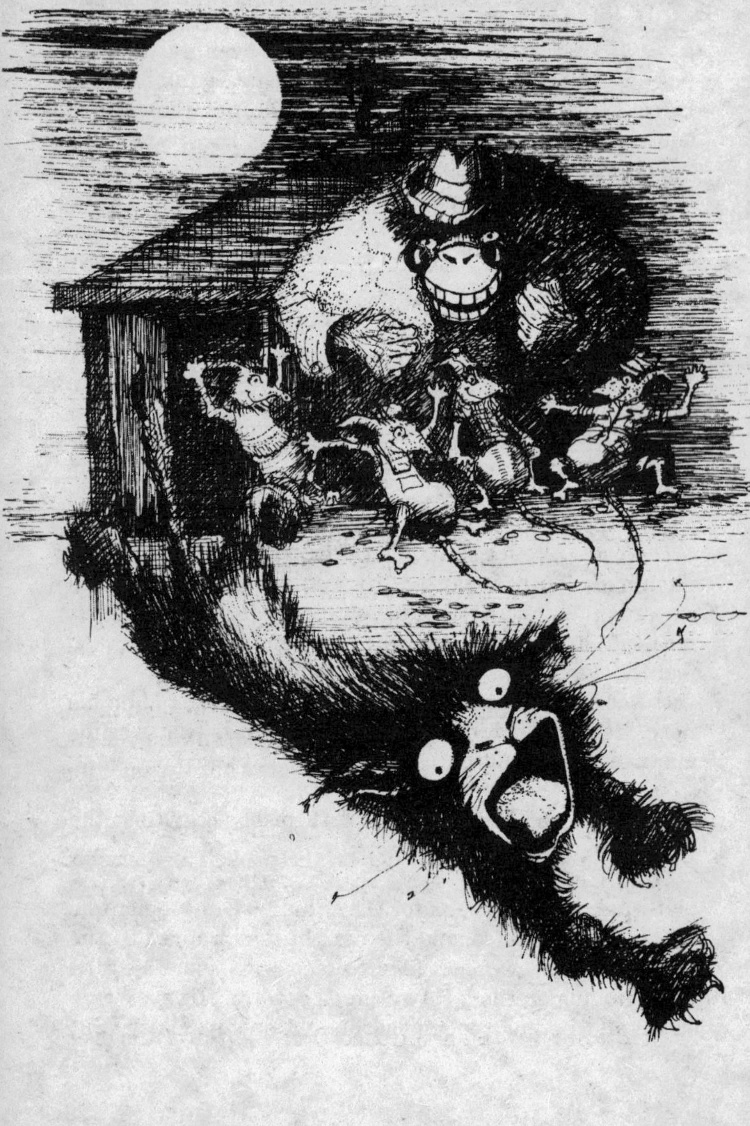

Batty had hopped to one side and pointed at him – and shouted.

"Cat!"

Suddenly, instead of Batty, there was a hairy monster with teeth which gleamed white, even in the dark. He had no idea what it was, and no time to work it out, but it was fierce and terrible and coming for him – growling. He shivered, but then, trapped though he was, he showed his own teeth and spat.

It was what they expected him to do. If he had smiled it would not have worked. Batty wanted him furious – and he was.

The monster, still growling leaned closer, until Oily Sludge could see the pink gums arching over the teeth.

"Now!" Sid shouted and the rats suddenly leaped clear.

Because Oily Sludge had been pushing with all his strength, the door flew open when they let go, and unable to stop, he exploded through it with legs flailing in all directions as he tried to get a grip on the ground. For a moment he was sure the jaws had him. He felt the hot breath. But it was not part of Batty's plan.

As Oily Sludge's claws bit into the ground, and as he gained some control of his legs, he threw himself at the monster. He had nowhere else to go.

The monster opened his legs and he went through them. Before he knew it he was on the other side, gulping for air, with his ears flat on his head and his paws hardly touching the ground.

Batty and the rats cheered him on. They jumped up and down and slapped each other on the back. They laughed and whistled after him. Their worst enemy was on the run.

"He goes a bit faster than yours, Sid." Orse was laughing so much he was choking.

"Faster than my what?"

"Faster than your cat on a string."

Sid flicked his tail and tipped Orse's hat over his eyes.

"Wouldn't want Oily Sludge on a string, would we?" he laughed. "But it worked, didn't it? He's minding us." He turned to the gorilla who was also laughing. "Smashing! Well done! You have to do that every time you see a cat. Remember . . . every time." He winked at Batty.

The gorilla nodded. He leaned on his knuckles, resting after the excitement, while Clappy slipped into the shed and came out with the chicken. They watched him strip it to the bones and throw the meat into the river. He put the bones back inside the shed. "A consolation present for Oily Sludge," he said, "for when he comes back."

"If he comes back." Totters laughed.

The others laughed as well but Batty, sitting slightly apart from them, was not so sure. He was pleased Operation Minder had started well, but he knew they had a lot to do yet. He had the feeling, because he could put himself in the enemy's place, that they were not finished with Oily Sludge. His neck would be painful. He deserved that, but he would recover and he would be back looking for revenge.

Batty turned towards the bright lights across the river. It was a good start. Oily Sludge was miles away – probably still running. Now it was time for a night out.

Chapter Six

Soho, close to Piccadilly Circus in the centre of London, has many restaurants, and one of them is specially popular with the Battersea gang because the food is good and because it is on a corner with a dark alley at the side.

It was busy when they arrived. The windows were steamed up, and they could hear the buzz of chatter and the rattle of plates. It sounded good as Weston steered the gorilla past the entrance and into the alley.

After fixing Oily Sludge they had crossed the river again, over Chelsea Bridge – the proper way like ordinary people. Just before the bridge they came to a coffee-stall with bright lights. The gorilla stopped and sniffed.

Batty popped his head out of the scarf. "Not here," he whispered. "Don't stop. The food's terrible."

It was not exactly true because he knew that the bread and cheese would be fresh, but he did not want to risk everything just for a snack and a cup of coffee.

Fortunately the stall-keeper was busy preparing for the evening, and he did not look twice at someone who was not a regular customer.

There was a plate of cheese rolls on the counter, and the gorilla helped himself to a couple. It could have been a difficult moment, but to Batty's surprise he did it like an expert. He waited until the stall-keeper turned away. Then his hand flashed up and back down to his side, with the rolls well out of sight.

They stopped on the bridge. The reflected lights attracted the gorilla, and he leaned over to get a better look at the water. It was a bad moment for Totters and Orse who were riding in a shopping bag. When they looked out they found they were dangling in space, with nothing between themselves and the river below. It was a long drop, and they hardly dared move in case they startled him and he let go of the bag.

"Batty. . ." Orse cried out.

"What's up?"

"Look where we are."

"It's nothing," said Batty. "He's just stopped to eat his rolls. He's hungry."

"Hungry!" Totters had his teeth clamped on the gorilla's sleeve. "Never mind his appetite. What about us?" His voice was muffled because he dare not let go.

The gorilla seemed to sense his panic and immediately lifted the bag to safety.

They went on again, past the barracks where the sentry at the gate did not give them a second look. Nor did anyone they passed bother with an old man wrapped up against the cold and going home with his shopping.

The gorilla smiled to himself. He knew he was doing well. But he had to be careful and listen all the time, and he had to remember to walk upright even when he wanted to lean on his knuckles.

"The Queen lives there," Batty explained as they passed Buckingham Palace. "She's queen of all of us – you as well now."

There were leaves on the pavement. He would have

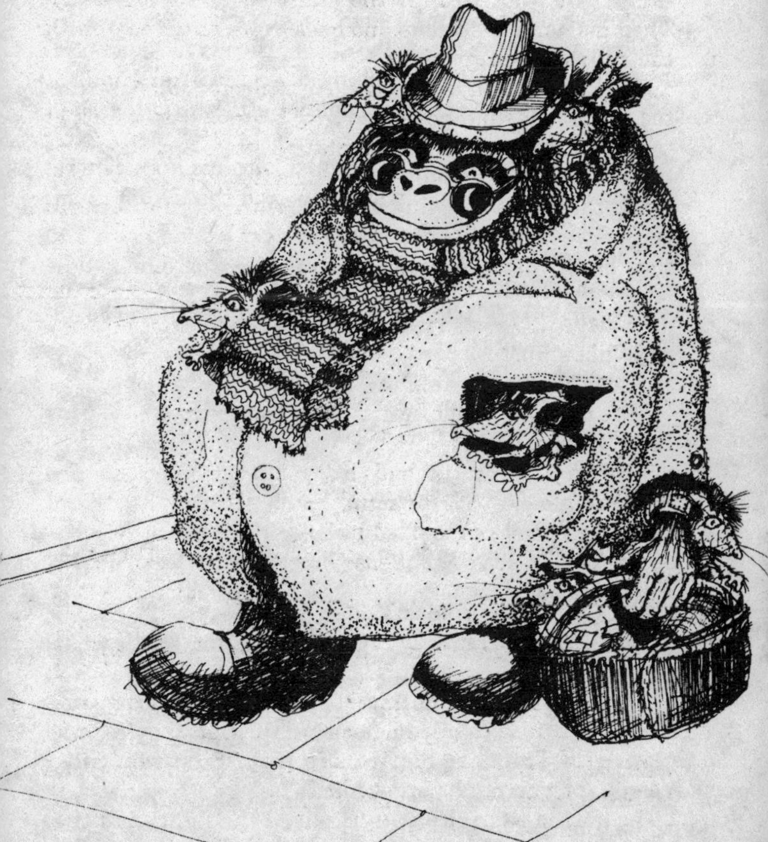

liked to walk through them with nothing on his feet.

In a place called Trafalgar Square they took a rest. He was glad to settle on a bench with his shopping bag on his lap, and he remembered to keep his feet on the ground and his chin well down in the scarf.

It was Weston who gave the alarm. He had his head just out of the scarf, camouflaged in the gorilla's hair, and as soon as he whistled the rat-warning Batty was at his side.

"What's up?"

"Over there . . ." Weston pointed with his nose. There was a policeman and policewoman, and the two of them were looking straight at the gorilla.

"They could be on to us."

"You mean the law? Don't worry. They're always here. They're on duty." Batty stayed calm, but kept his eyes on the police, ready to act.

"But look Batty . . ." Weston nudged him.

"I am looking. They haven't twigged him."

"Not him . . . look over there."

"Where?"

"The paper-man. See what it says?"

"What does it say?"

Weston read the words out loud, "GORILLA . . . HUNT . . . LATEST . . ."

"So what's the problem?"

"It's in the papers. They're hunting for him. That's what it says."

"Of course they're hunting – of course it's in the papers. They don't lose a gorilla every day. But they're not hunting in Trafalgar Square, are they? Stop worrying, Weston, or you might upset him."

The gorilla sat quite still. He liked the lights and the fountains spraying water, and all the people – some of them walking, and some like him, just sitting and looking. It was good to rest with his feet in his own boots and with a coat and hat like other people. He was not worried by the words on the news-stand.

Then the police started to walk towards him. He tensed, but although he was ready he stayed quite still, like his friends in his scarf, and waited.

The policewoman stared at him and smiled. The old man was probably tired, but he was not in any sort of trouble. She had sharp eyes but an old man dozing on a public bench was not unusual. The gorilla smiled back as they walked past.

* * *

The alley was deserted. There was nothing there for the evening crowd, just offices locked up for the night, and at the back of the restaurant – dustbins and sacks of rubbish. Nobody was interested in the alley — except for Batty and the rats who used it regularly.

It was not stale food that interested them. They were not scavengers. What brought them there was a side window, fixed so that it appeared closed, although they could open it whenever they wanted.

It let them into a back staircase which was never used by the restaurant customers. Clappy had it all sorted out. The panelling on the side of the staircase covered a lift-shaft going from the restaurant to a basement kitchen. He had one of the panels hinged so that when they opened it they could get at the lift. It was a small lift on ropes, and it went up and down all the time the restaurant was busy.

Since he had fixed the hinges they could use the restaurant whenever they liked, setting up their own table on the stairs. They used a broom-handle pushed through the ropes to stop the lift. Sometimes they helped themselves from the full plates going up. And sometimes Weston slipped into the lift with a pencil and altered the orders going down to the kitchen so they had whole plates of food specially to themselves. It was a foolproof system. They could even stop the lift on the way down and get rid of their empty plates – and it was all free.

Tonight it was the gorilla's turn. They could not expect him yet to walk into a restaurant and sit down. He was not ready for that. But he was ready for a good dinner, and they had him hidden in an office in the alley, out of sight behind drawn blinds, sitting at a desk with a clean napkin tucked in his scarf.

Totters and Orse were waiting on him. They were doing it properly, and although his table manners were still terrible they served him with as much care as he would have got from the waiters in the restaurant.

The spaghetti and salad should have been eaten separately, but he liked the colours mixed together, and the lettuce leaves helped him pick up the spaghetti. Batty supervised his dinner like a head-waiter, making sure he had everything he wanted.

Weston and Clappy were on the broom-handle. It was a hectic time. The gorilla ate quickly, and he ate a lot. At the end of dinner they were staggering. They had worked non-stop and had not had a proper dinner themselves. When they had the chance they had snatched bits from the plates going up to the restaurant, but they had had to eat while they worked. It was hard but it was all in a good cause. They had to show their minder what they could do for him.

The gorilla enjoyed himself. He was used to having his meals brought to him, but he had never had a dinner like this. As soon as he emptied his plate there was another one in front of him. He ate everything, and when he had had enough he sat back and banged on his stomach. When he saw Batty frowning at the mess he had made he understood at once. He should have been more careful. He smiled and licked the desk top until there was not a crumb on it, and afterwards he wiped it dry with his sleeve.

Batty stopped frowning and nodded approvingly. They had to be sure not to leave any evidence. When he saw the desk was clean Batty slipped away for a moment to organise the others. It was soon after this that things began to go unexpectedly wrong.

Chapter Seven

It was after breakfast, with Bennett safely away to the market and with the gorilla washed and comfortable in his armchair. Weston was brushing the overcoat when he started finding things in the pockets. There was a bag with a powder compact and a lipstick in a gold case, a brush and comb and a box with scented soap. There were plastic earrings, a nail-file and red varnish. "Look at this lot, Batty." He placed them on the table as they appeared. "A bottle of pills, a packet of mints. . ."

Batty examined each article. He was frowning but the gorilla went on picking grape pips from his teeth.

"No wonder we had an uncomfortable ride back. We were on top of that lot." Sid pointed. "A paper punch and a stapler, I was sitting on 'em."

"Me too." Orse picked up the punch and let it fall on the table. "I was sitting on that all the way home." He looked hard at the gorilla. "You pinched this lot, didn't you?

From the desk where you had your dinner. You thieved it?"

The gorilla smiled.

Weston spoke in a worried whisper. "He's light-fingered, Batty. He pinches things. We didn't think of that."

The gorilla seemed about to pick something from the table, but Batty flicked his tail to stop him. "You could get into trouble for this," he said, "trouble with the law. You have to be careful when you pinch things."

Orse poked about among the things on the table. "And it's got to be worth pinching. We can't do much with this lot."

Batty cleared a space and faced the gorilla. He put his thumbs in his braces. "Shoplifting . . ." he spoke seriously, "taking things from offices is the same as shoplifting, gets people into trouble. They get nicked . . . arrested. You don't want to get nicked, do you? You don't want to be locked up again?" He was thinking hard. They had to make the gorilla understand. He whispered to Weston to fetch a pencil and paper. "You're a gorilla," he went on, "or were before we started changing you. And when you were a gorilla you had a ticket on your cage . . . like this." He pointed to the paper. "Write it down, Weston, write gorilla."

Weston wrote.

"But you're light-fingered. Perhaps all gorillas are light-fingered . . . perhaps not. So we'll write that down."

Weston licked his pencil.

"See what it says now? Read it out, Weston." Batty waited a moment. "We're working hard to change you, aren't we? And you'll have to work hard. You'll have to behave better or you'll get nicked and locked up again. You've got to remember that, so we'll stick the ticket on the wall for a bit to remind you." He pointed. "Put it up there, Sid, on the nail."

The writing stood out clearly.

> A lite fingerd Goriller

"We'll leave it for a few days," Batty snapped his braces. "It'll remind you that thieving's dangerous, and you have to be careful not to get caught."

"Alf!" Weston shouted and they all jumped.

"Who?"

"Alf... it's him." Weston pointed at the paper and then at the gorilla.

"Who?"

"Alf... it's Alf..." He sprang across to the wall and made marks on the paper. "Look..." He underlined the three letters, "A...l...f... it spells a name. Read the letters I've put a line under and you get a name, Alf... Alf Gorilla."

"Alf..."

"Alf..."

"A light-fingered gorilla called Alf."

They tried the name out on each other and then on the gorilla who banged his stomach and looked pleased.

"He likes it..."

"It suits him..."

"My grandad was called Alf," said Orse, "and he had black hair."

They tried it out some more, calling him from different parts of the arch so that he turned when he heard the name. They decided it was good because they could talk to him properly now, and a name made him more human. It was another step forward.

* * *

"Not that one, Alf." It was later in the day, lesson time again. "This one," Batty explained, "the one with the black knob."

They were in the Sludge-Gulper, a rusty old tanker lorry with a pipe for sucking which was kept parked on the wharf. They were showing him how to work it. It was not comfortable like a proper car, but it was on the spot and the rats knew all about it. They had spent many hours under an oily rag in the cab watching the driver. They had, in a way, named Oily Sludge after it.

It was deserted on the wharf at this time in the evening, and Alf was having his first driving lesson. They worked as a team.

Batty encouraged him. "That's right . . . the black knob . . . you have to pull it to start up." He tapped Alf's hand. "Go on . . . you do it."

Alf jumped as the motor turned.

"Keep pulling till it starts properly," Batty shouted. "Slap his foot, Clappy."

Alf let go of the knob and put both hands on the steering wheel.

"Not yet . . ." Sid sat beside him, in charge of the handbrake. "You don't steer till we're moving."

"Not till the motor's running . . . like this. I'll do it for you." Batty pulled the starter for him.

Clappy down on the floor, slapped Alf's foot. "Push the pedal down now," he shouted.

The motor rattled and began to roar.

"Off!" Clappy kicked the foot. "You only have to push a bit . . . gently, not hard down all the time."

The motor was running: phut . . . phut . . . phut . . .

thump, and they were all shaking, but Alf quickly understood. His hat slipped over his eyes but he was not worried. He let Weston put it straight and concentrated hard on what he had to do.

Clappy kicked his foot again. "He's got it, Batty," he shouted. "He's beginning to get the feel."

"Let's try moving then . . . just a bit in bottom gear."

There was a clunk as Totters worked Alf's other foot on the clutch pedal and Weston pushed in the gear lever.

"Go . . ."

The Sludge-Gulper jerked forward in a cloud of smoke and knocked over Bennett's celery bath. It squashed the celery and stopped on the edge of the wharf. Sid, with Orse and Battty, was on the handbrake doing an emergency stop.

Weston looked out of the side window. "We're nearly in the river, Batty."

Batty stayed calm. "You have to do it slowly, Alf," he explained, "take your foot off the pedal gently when you start. Let's have another go . . . backwards this time. Totters, help him with his foot . . . hold it down. Weston, move the lever for him . . . for going backwards."

They tried again and managed to stop with only a light crunch on the wall. Alf liked it and wanted to go on, but Batty decided it was enough. They had made a lot of noise – Alf kept pushing too hard – and they had to get Bennett's celery cleared up. He stood by while Alf lifted the bath up the right way and the others put back the celery. They chattered as they worked. It was going to be all right. They were sure Alf could learn to drive the Sludge-Gulper. Then they could go anywhere. It was an exciting prospect. But in their excitement they were unusually careless, and none of them, not even Batty saw the eyes watching them.

The eyes were closed to narrow slits so that they reflected nothing, and as the gang cleared up and peace returned to the wharf they backed slowly away into the dark.

Oily Sludge no longer felt sorry for himself. He smiled in fact for the first time in days as he slipped silently away into the night.

Chapter Eight

Bennett jumped up and down on a box, making the splinters fly. There had to be something he could do. His celery was squashed and there was more fruit missing. It was worse every day. He had to find a way of getting rid of the rats.

"Robbers! Thieves! I'll murder you!"

Suddenly he was quiet. He looked up. If they were up there, where the pipes ran across the ceiling, he could make them fall into boiling water, or wet cement, or better still tar. They deserved to drown in hot tar.

"Just wait!" he shouted, "just you wait!"

They heard him from next door, but Alf was used to him by now, and got on with his breakfast. The rats were busy getting ready for a special day. Alf was a front-page fugitive. He was in all the papers. But he had made so much progress that Batty decided they could risk taking him out for the first time in daylight.

They spent the morning on a special lesson. Alf had to learn about money. Money had never bothered them before. Nobody sold anything to rats. But as he became

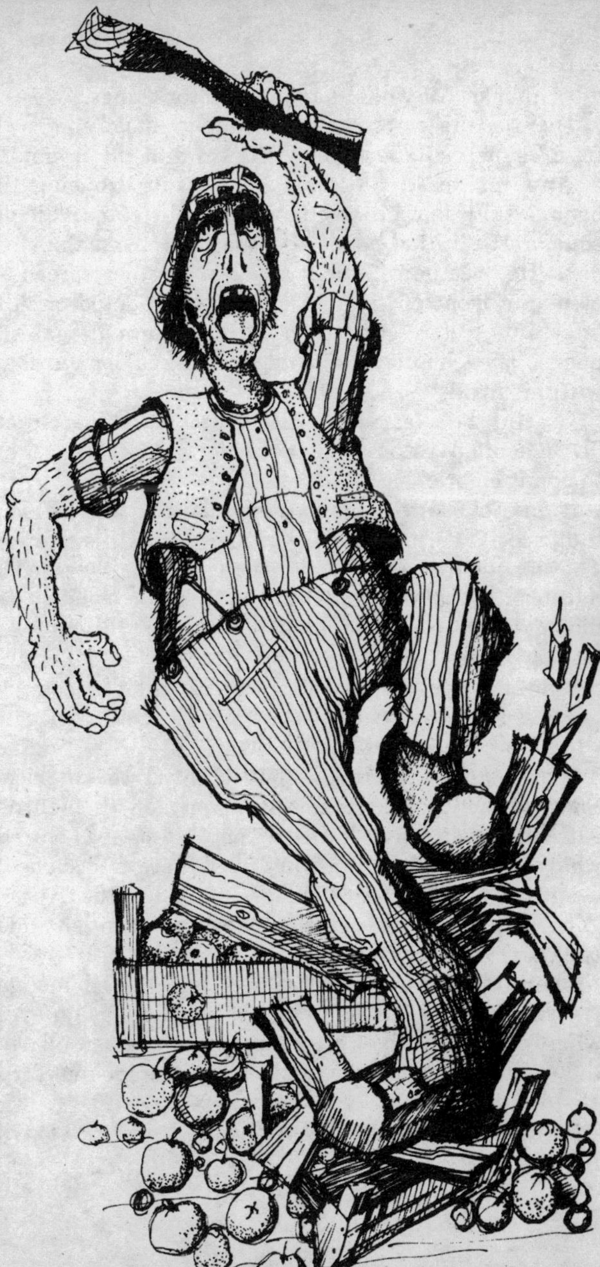

more human Alf would have to pay for things.

They had the lesson ready, with money mostly borrowed from Bennett's loose change. Alf was difficult at first. He was not interested in notes. Paper was for dropping, like banana skins, but he was happy with the coins which he could rattle in his hand, and specially liked the shiny ones. He tried hard to understand when they spread the money in front of him. When Weston counted on Alf's fingers up to ten – and then did it again and again, he nodded at each number and tried to make the right shape with his lips.

"I think he's learning." Batty was watching closely. "Do it again, Weston. It's not easy for him. He's never had to count before."

It was not easy but they were patient. So was Alf. They took special care when they groomed him this morning. They made sure he washed properly, and they brushed his hair over his ears so that Batty and Weston could be well hidden when they went out. They cleaned his boots and his sunglasses.

They all paid special attention to their appearance because Batty reckoned that if they all looked smart Alf would follow their example.

When they were ready they climbed the barricade together and sorted themselves out for the journey. Although it was day Alf was not shy. He stepped onto the wharf as though he had always lived there, and sucked in deep breaths of fresh air. The special smell of the river was good, and a chest full of air helped him pull his shoulders back and stand upright.

They started at the market and Batty kept his fingers crossed. By now the hunt for the gorilla was on everywhere and there might be extra police out – as well as all the ordinary people who could be on the lookout for an escaped gorilla.

He need not have worried. Alf had no intention of giving

himself away. He gripped the shopping bag, kept his chin down and shuffled into the crowd. He took an interest in everything. He watched what other people did – and did the same. At some stalls he stopped and looked closely at what was on sale. He even stopped in front of Bennett's. He recognised the voice when he was offered a pineapple cheap, but he was careful to do nothing.

Riding in the bag or in the pockets was dangerous. The rats had to be prepared all the time for falling objects. Alf was still helping himself to anything he fancied. It worried Batty who as usual was watching everything he did, but he seemed to have a natural cunning which protected him. He took things only when he was sure it was safe.

He had worked it out. When he saw something he fancied, perhaps a bag of sweets, he stopped and smiled as though he was a customer. When he got a smile back he changed suddenly and put on one of his fierce looks, just showing his teeth. It always worked. The surprised stall-owner always looked away.

The first bag of sweets dropped unexpectedly hard on Totters and stunned him for a moment. But he realised what was happening and he was ready for the next delivery.

When they left the market Alf's pockets and the shopping bag were nearly full, and he still had a purse full of money. Weston shook his head, but they all enjoyed the sweets, even when they went up the hill past the police-station and the magistrate's court.

It was a bright day, almost cold, with an east wind which blew uncomfortably up the side roads. But they were all warm. The shopping bag was as good as an anorak, and the coat pockets were lined with soft material. Alf was specially warm with his own fur coat under the overcoat.

He was beginning to understand now about walking in the streets. All he had to do was watch other people. He had to remember to stop before he crossed the road, and listen to Weston. "Look left . . . look right . . ." He got it in the proper order sometimes.

At the big roads he had to stop and cross at a special place. It was easy. He waited with the other people and went when they did. When he reached Clapham Common at last and stepped onto the grass, and saw what was ahead he started to hurry. There was something special happening and he wanted to be there.

Chapter Nine

"It's thirty pence . . . three coins . . . the large silver ones," Weston whispered urgently. "Don't pinch it. You have to buy it." They were crossing the Common in a crowd, mostly of adults being hurried along by children. "Thirty pence."

Alf stopped. His nostrils twitched.

"Get your candy-floss here . . ."

Weston was so anxious he almost bit Alf's ear. "Use the purse . . . take out the money . . . pay for it."

A clown on stilts towered over them blowing a trumpet. A midget with a drum skipped between his legs.

"Pay for it . . . three of the silver ones . . ."

The drum beat kept the crowd moving.

As Alf grabbed the candy-floss the man hardly noticed. He took coins from the black palm, and had already forgotten this customer as he twisted a new stick in the spinning sugar.

Alf pointed his lips to touch it. It was a lovely colour and sticky, and when he licked it off it melted on his tongue and tasted good.

Batty leaned over and gave Weston a thumbs-up. It had been a tricky moment but Alf had managed. He had understood how to hold out his money just like other people.

The candy-floss was worth thirty pence. It was a sort of prize for Alf, and even better it hid most of his face. He played with it with the tip of his tongue as Weston steered him into the queue for the circus. The next test was buying the ticket.

There are lots of things to look at when you go to the circus, and no one noticed Weston wriggle down Alf's arm and help him take more coins from the purse. Alf watched what was happening, and when he held out the money he got a ticket.

He would have thrown it away. It was only paper. But the other people were holding theirs and he kept it until it was taken from him. When he gave it up he was led to a seat. It was in the front, his own chair, and he remembered to keep his feet on the ground. The rats sorted themselves out so that they could see. Clappy and Sid slipped into the shopping bag on Alf's lap so that there were four noses sticking out, with a perfect view of the ring.

Alf was busy with his candy-floss as the circus started. There was music and a man with a whistle – and suddenly very bright lights. There were horses with feathers on their heads. They ran round and round and made a lot of dust. The lights changed colour and there were people just in front of him, making everyone laugh. He could have joined in. They were rolling about. He began to move.

"Sit still . . . they're called clowns." Weston explained. "They're only pretending to fall over."

The tallest one was going to knock the smallest one down.

"It's a pretend hammer . . . don't worry."

But the little one winked at Alf and poked his umbrella between the big one's legs. He fell down in front of Alf and shouted while the little one beat him with his umbrella.

"It's not real," Weston whispered urgently. "They're friends really . . . like us. They're just playing."

Alf settled back in his seat. He slapped his stomach because he saw everyone was clapping. The lights changed again and pointed upwards. When he looked up there was someone in shiny clothes climbing to the top of a pole and swaying over him. And another one who hung by her teeth and twirled round and round so high that he had to hold onto his hat when he leaned back to watch. He liked the high bits.

The music changed. He recognised the animals when they came in. He had seen elephants before with children riding on their backs, but these were different. They were better. They had special clothes, coloured and sparkling, and they could walk on two legs like people. Everyone clapped when they did that.

When the clowns came back in a car he liked it a lot, especially when it rattled and fell to pieces.

The lights pointed upwards again. There were more people climbing, with clothes which sparkled in the light.

"And now, ladies and gentlemen . . ." The voice came from all around. There was more clapping and cheers. "Ladies and gentlemen . . . what you've all been waiting for . . . the amazing death-defying flying . . ." The cheering drowned out the words.

The sparkling people climbed to a place high up, and stood in the bright lights and waved down. Alf waved back. Suddenly one of them was flying like a bird, higher and higher. He was hanging by his hands, and then he was sitting, flying and waving.

Alf heard Batty and Weston gasp as the man stretched his arms wide – and fell.

But not far. He stopped suddenly. The screams were cut off. The man was still flying, hanging upside down. The lights picked out another one, a girl. She waved and leaned forward and jumped. Her hair trailed behind her. She was flying by herself, turning over in the air, then her fingers touched the other one and they were flying together. Alf breathed again.

The drum started, soft then louder and faster. Alf risked a quick glance sideways. Every eye was looking up. The drum stopped.

"Ladies and gentlemen, the amazing triple somersault. . ."

It started again. Alf tapped out the rhythm, faster and faster. Screams drowned the drumming. She was falling, really falling – not flying. It was a long way. She spread her arms as she fell. Then she hit – and bounced, and bounced again. Alf could have held her.

It was too much. He was out of his seat. He knew what to do. He grabbed the ladder and climbed easily, holding the shopping bag in his teeth. He did not bother with his feet. He made the right shape with his fingers, hooked them on the ladder and used his muscles. It was easy. As he climbed he could hear the people cheering. They were watching him. He would go right to the top for them.

It was high up there, and there was hardly room for his feet. But when he reached the standing place he held the shopping bag properly and remembered to stand upright.

"Stop it, Alf!"

"Pack it in!" Batty and Weston were shouting.

From where he stood it was a long way down to the faces, but he was not worried. He swayed as though he was about to fall, and the noise rushed up at him. He swung his arms to keep his balance.

At that moment Orse untangled himself from the others and looked out of the shopping bag. The lights rushed by – and the white faces stared up. His stomach turned over. It was dark, then light again. Everything was going round. He shut his eyes – he was getting dizzy – and risked opening them for another look. A moment ago they had been part of a happy crowd, safe in their ringside seat. Now it looked dangerous.

Alf was too busy to worry about danger. Someone kept the spotlight on him so that the audience could see everything. They saw an old man who tugged his hat on and made sure his sunglasses stayed on his nose. They loved it, especially when he pretended to lose his balance and had to swing his shopping round his head to stay upright.

Then he was flying. Alf saw the bar swinging towards him. It was easy to lean out and grab it.

There was no going back after that. The air rushed by but he was not falling. He was flying upwards – gripping tight. He was safe.

At the top he stopped for an instant, lying on his back in the air. Then he was flying backwards. He looked over his shoulder. It was easy. He grunted happily as he flew backwards and forwards and heard the people cheering. He put the bag in his teeth again and waved. With two hands on the bar he found he could swing higher by leaning out and stretching. He could go right up into the dark beyond the lights. The people would like that. Alf saw there were places up there which he could reach and use. He swung harder and higher.

Batty and Weston were in shock. It was impossible to talk to Alf. It was as much as they could do to breathe. They had to hang on with their mouths open, wondering what he would do next.

Alf showed them. He let go of the bar, grabbed for the dark and stayed there while the empty trapeze swung back. Without pausing he was off again, moving easily hand over hand along the high trellis of the big top.

When the lights picked him up he held his hat on and jumped again. It was not a good moment for Batty and the rats. Their stomachs were full of sweets and were the wrong way up most of the time, and hanging on was difficult. One moment they were zooming up or down, and the next they jarred to a sudden stop. Then they were off again as Alf looked for new tricks.

He used his strong arms to force the trapeze higher, let go in mid-air, twisted and caught another trapeze. The crowd roared as he swung himself into the dark, and became quiet as they followed the vague shape moving about right at the top of the tent.

"Pack it up, Alf." The pause was just long enough for Batty to get his breath back. "You'll kill us."

Alf grunted. They were safe enough and he was enjoying himself, but Batty sounded angry. He climbed down to the platform where it had all started. The cheering and clapping stopped, and the silence told him they were waiting down there. He smiled at them and waved – and stepped into space.

This time he really fell, but he knew what he was doing. He had seen what happened to the girl. He fell with his arms waving and with his feet running as though he was trying desperately to climb up again. He laughed out loud and held his hat on as he thumped into the net. He bounced higher than the girl because he was heavier, and kept bouncing. The crowd roared.

"Marvellous . . ." The ring-master was standing with the circus boss. "He's marvellous . . . fantastic. Where did you find him?"

"I didn't find him." The boss mopped his brow. He had been expecting an accident. "Who is he?"

"You mean you don't know him? You didn't book him?" asked the ring-master.

"Of course I didn't. I thought you had."

"Not me. I've never seen him before. But he's a great act." The ring-master was delighted with the applause which went on and on. He had heard stories of amateurs who would try any trick to get into the circus. This must be one of them.

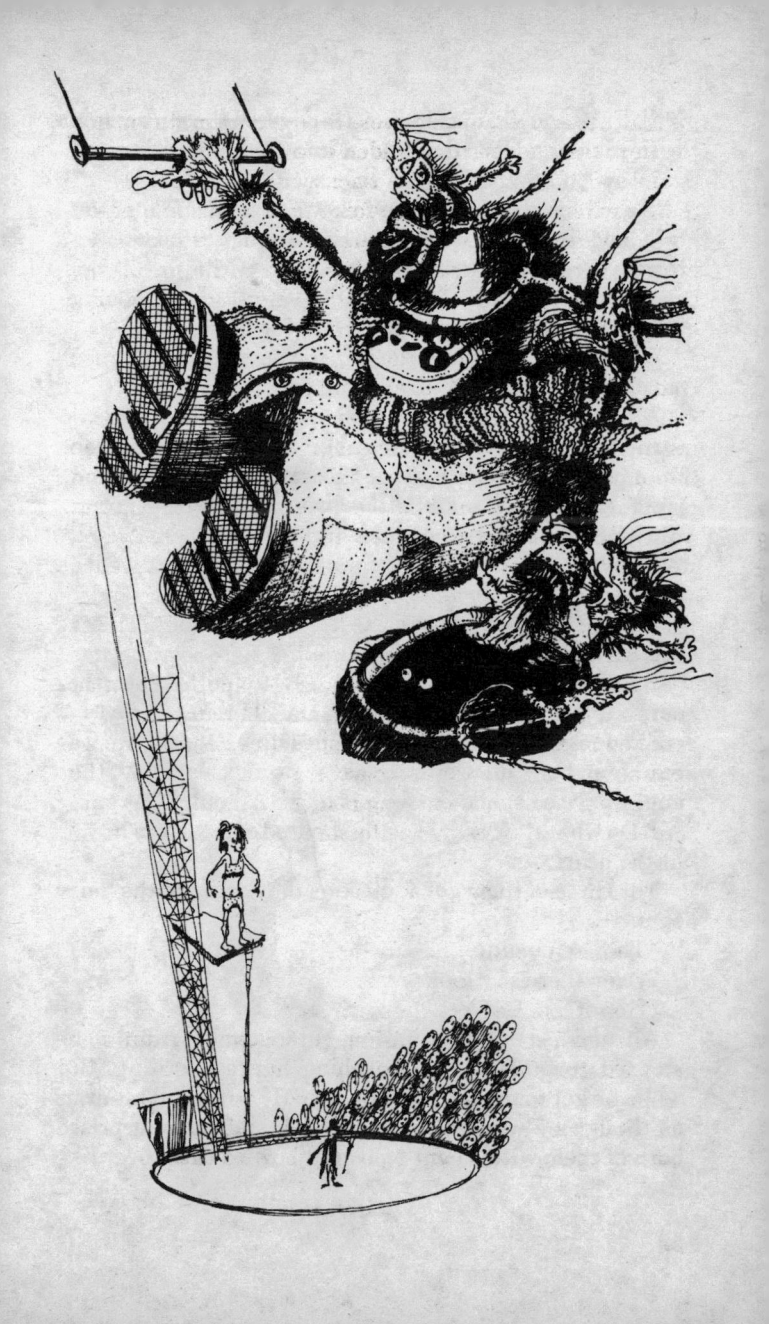

"Ladies and gentlemen . . ." He covered the microphone with his hand. "We don't even know his name."

"How could we? We've never seen him before."

"Listen to them cheering. They like him. He's good."

"Good! He's inhuman." The boss shook his head. "He's terrific. Nobody climbs like that."

"He does."

The audience stamped their feet for more.

"Well don't just stand there." The boss pushed the ringmaster forward. "Get him. Bring him to me."

Alf bounced once more, grabbed the edge of the net, turned a somersault and landed on the sawdust. He stood for a moment, slightly out of breath, but he was smiling.

As soon as they realised they were back on the ground Batty and Weston went into action. "Scarper, Alf . . " Batty was as alarmed as he sounded. "Quick . . . or we'll be in trouble."

Weston grabbed his ear. "Out, Alf . . . get out. They're coming for us."

"Out . . . quick, Alf . . . out . . ." Batty pulled the other ear, but Alf stood still, enjoying the clapping.

Sid untangled himself and slipped up Alf's arm. He was ready, as they all were, to make a quick exit, but they might have a second or two left to get Alf out. "Get going Alf. Do what Batty says . . ." he shouted even before he was in the scarf.

The three of them got as close as they could to the hairy ears.

"They're coming . . ."

"Over there . . . look . . ."

"Hop it . . . fast . . ."

Alf summed up the situation, but instead of running he stepped towards the approaching figures, smiling. But when he got to them he did not stop. He stretched his arms as though he wanted to greet them, and then surprised both of them with a gentle push. It bowled them over like skittles, and as they lay on the sawdust he stepped between them. The crowd thought it was part of the act and shouted for more.

"Don't stop . . . don't stop for anyone." The rats did not give Alf time to think. "Go . . . straight on . . . get out . . . that way . . . through the entrance . . ."

When they were outside they did not bother to let him carry them. They were on the ground, running. "Follow us . . . keep going . . . don't stop." They showed him the way under lorries and over fences. "This way . . . through here . . . quick . . ."

They scrambled over the last fence together. Alf was laughing and holding his hat on, and when they were heading for the main road the rats began laughing with him. The panic was over.

"A flying gorilla . . . we've got a flying gorilla, Batty." Totters was puffing and skipping. "The only flying gorilla in the world and we've got him. We could join the circus." He risked a look back. "I bet they're still talking about him."

"And clapping." Orse was trying to keep his hat on.

"You were good, Alf," Clappy shouted, "very good."

"Too good!" Sid helped Batty onto Alf's shoulder. "But don't ever do that again." Batty hung on and shouted.

"Never again, Alf . . . understand."

Alf was happy. He had shown them all what he could do.

"You won't ever do it again, will you, Alf?"

Alf nodded as Batty and Weston wriggled back into the scarf. He slowed down when they reached the road and took special care to walk upright.

Chapter Ten

There were a lot of people trying to get the gorilla back. But according to the flags pinned in the map at the zoo there could have been as many as sixty gorillas roaming around the south of England.

"If we believe all the reports," the Director was talking to the press, "there must be more gorillas in England than there are in Africa."

He liked all animals, especially wild ones. It was part of his job. But he had a special liking for the big apes. He sometimes thought he preferred them to humans, and he was confident his gorilla would soon find his own way back. In the zoo the gorilla was warm and well looked after. Outside he would be cold and would be missing the meals he got regularly, especially the fresh fruit.

* * *

At the circus they were not thinking about gorillas. They were thinking about the old man who had appeared at the matinee and worked himself into the trapeze act. They wondered who it could have been and then decided it was not an old man at all. He was too good. It had to be someone from another circus playing a joke on them. It was a trick they had all heard about.

* * *

Bennett was his usual grumpy self. His feet ached. His hands were stiff from handling muddy potatoes. His ears were cold. His nose was running – and the rats were still in his store.

* * *

Oily Sludge was also thinking about rats – and revenge. He had been going over plans as he rubbed ointment on his neck, and although he preferred to work alone he had come to the conclusion that he needed help. He needed a gang, a commando of tough cats like himself. If they worked together and chose the right moment they could get rid of the rats for good.

The problem was the monster. He wondered how much help he would need to get rid of that. He rubbed his neck again, taking special care that the movement did not give him away.

* * *

The rats had gone straight home after the circus. Their performance in it had left them excited, once they got over the shock. To fly through the air on a trapeze, even in a shopping bag, was special. They would never have dared to do anything like it. It was also a triumph.

Alf had been right in the spotlight, in full view of the public, with all eyes on him, and he had not been found out. They had made a quick getaway afterwards, but there had been no sign of a chase, no police sirens or flashing lights. Of all the people who had been looking, none of them had linked him with the missing gorilla, even though there were pictures of him in all the papers. They could hardly have thought up a better test for him.

"But you've got to be more careful." Batty sat on Alf's bed. "We know you're clever. We know you can do lots of things. That's why we got you. But you have to be careful all the time or you might get caught and sent back to the zoo. If that happens they'll put you in a cage again, and they'll put stronger locks on it, probably a special guard so you won't get out again. You won't be free like you are now. You'll be sad and miserable. And we'll be sad too – all of us."

Alf lay back and peeled another banana. Weston was brushing his coat, and they were all busy and in high spirits.

"It's time," Batty winked at Sid. "We'll drop in on Oily Sludge again on the way – give him another dose of the medicine."

Sid slipped across to the wardrobe. He picked up his string and pulled, and they all jumped and shouted.

"Cat!"

"Cat!"

"Cat!"

Alf bounced on the bed growling and showing his teeth. The old cat was better than an alarm clock.

"Smashing!" Batty was satisfied. "Always remember to do that, Alf – as soon as you hear us shout."

* * *

They were out of luck when they came to the shed. Oily Sludge was not at home. Sid crept up to the door and tapped gently, while the others crouched ready. There was no answer. Oily Sludge was not in the shed. He was outside, right behind them.

Earlier, when they came out of the arch together, he pressed close to the ground and held his breath. An old man, he thought, not a monster at all. It's just an old man with big teeth. It would be easy.

He watched Sid tap on his door again, and then silently left them to it.

Batty decided not to wait. Oily Sludge had been their first target, but there were plenty of other cats. Any cat would do.

The next one they found never really recovered from the experience. She was from a good home, not a wharf cat. She was well looked after and spent a comfortable life, mostly on cushions or on a warm lap. It was her bad luck to be stepping out of her door at just the wrong moment.

Sid was scouting ahead along a wall to see if there was anything interesting on the other side. "Freeze!" He rat-whistled the warning as he caught the flash of cat eyes.

"Aiyeee . . . ooo . . . ooo . . . owww . . ."

It was the right noise, a low note stretching up the scale and back down to the same note. Sid made it by pinching his nose and opening and closing his mouth.

The cat did not have any appointments for the evening and was not expecting visitors, but it was a proper cat noise. It had to be one of her friends. She held back a little, as a well-bred cat should, and Sid called again. The rest of them stayed out of sight. Sid moaned invitingly. He knew how to make any cat sound.

The cat brushed the air with her tail but kept her head turned away, as though she was not interested. She was in no hurry. But suddenly she changed her mind. She sensed a movement in the shadows. There was a whistle, scuffling – screaming.

"Cat!"

"Cat! Cat!"

She did not have a chance. She was suddenly paralysed. When she tried to step forward she found she could not move, but she had no way of knowing there were four rats holding her tail.

Normally, if anyone had dared insult her like this, she would have twisted and lunged. She would have scratched and might even have spat, but it all happened too quickly. She was suddenly face to face with a monster. It loomed over her, black with gleaming red eyes and big teeth, growling as it came for her.

Then she felt it. There was another behind her, standing on her tail. It was the moment to scream. She opened her mouth, and the cry was the signal. The rats let go. It was teamwork timed to the second. Suddenly freed, the cat sprang farther than she had ever sprung before. It could have been a record but she was not interested. She did not look back.

Sid pointed to the cat-door. "We can get in there, Batty." He looked up at the house. It had a cared-for, packed-with-food look, very promising. "I bet it's handsome inside. And it looks like no one's in. There's no lights. Shall we risk it?"

Batty nodded and pointed to Alf. "Don't forget we've got him."

"We'll open the door for him." It was no problem to Sid. "I'll go in first with Clappy and scout around. If it's safe we'll let him in."

They waited until the door flapped open again and Sid poked his nose out. "All clear." Totters and Orse slipped inside and they went to work on the back door. As soon as they had it open Batty and Weston hurried Alf inside. They closed the door behind him and stood empty bottles in front of the cat-flap in case the cat came back.

In the kitchen Weston showed Alf how to open the refrigerator. It was useful because with the door open they had enough light to be comfortable, and it was well-stocked.

They had a good dinner. Alf made his usual mess. Some things were easy to eat. He could pick them up, but there were sticky bits which stuck to his fingers and runny bits which kept slipping through them.

After dinner they took him into the best room and

switched on the television. He was happy sitting in an armchair. It was like home and he could wipe his fingers on the arms. But he was not sure about television. When Weston switched it on and he saw the picture he started a low growl. The picture disappeared. Then came back and went again. Weston passed the switch to him. "You press it."

Alf tried. He liked the way he could make the picture change, but just when he was getting used to it and they were preparing to settle down for the evening the police arrived. Orse was on guard at the window when the car stopped.

"Out!" He whistled the special warning and the rats did not ask questions. They went into action. They were in such a hurry that Totters tripped over the bottles by the back door, but they had it open for Alf who came out with Batty and Weston hanging round his neck like a fur collar.

"Down the garden . . ."

"Run . . ."

"Don't stop . . ."

"This is getting to be a habit . . ." Totters giggled as he beckoned Alf over the wall. "Don't look back . . ."

They were ten houses away by the time the police got round to the back and found the door open.

"Someone's working tonight." They looked inside.

"Or been careless – gone out and forgot to shut it."

They went in and looked over the house.

"Very careless – gone out and left the telly on."

"And the back door open . . ."

"And look at the mess in here . . ." They were in the kitchen.

"Imagine going out and leaving it like this. There's food all over the table . . ."

"And the floor . . ."

"Dirty people . . ."

"Deserve to get mice..."

"Or even rats..."

The policemen shook their heads. They searched the house and the garden, and decided it was just another false alarm. They went next door to the neighbours who had called them.

After the police left the neighbours thought about the noise they had heard, and remembered the cat. They often looked after her when her owners were away. But this time when they called her she did not appear. It was unusual. She always came when she was called.

Chapter Eleven

It rained all the next day and the well-behaved cat arrived home soaked. She was not a pretty sight. She waited a long time before she risked it, but when she was sure the monster was not there she let herself in.

She expected a warm welcome. She never stayed out all night, and she knew her owners would be worried and waiting for her, but she was not at all happy to find they were less concerned about her than they were about their own problems.

They could not understand it, they explained to the police. It was not their mess in the kitchen. They were clean people. Someone had been in the house, someone hungry.

Nor could they understand the open door. They were sure they had locked it. And the bottles inside were another mystery. They had not put them there. Added to all this was the robbery – the silver cigarette box. It was always on the table by the armchair, with matches. Now it was missing.

* * *

Unlike the owners of the cat, Bennett was feeling happy. He was putting his plan into action. It was brilliant, although Sid, lying out of sight and watching, did not think much of it.

Bennett had arrived early with a number of large plastic bins which he set out among the fruit and vegetables. He filled each bin to the top with water and then floated apples on it so that the whole surface was covered. Bennett was so confident of success that he was using his best apples, knowing he could sell them afterwards.

He had worked it out. A rat would jump onto the apples which would part unexpectedly and plunge him into deep water, and then close over him. He had a happy picture in his mind of rats trapped under the apples with nothing to grip on the smooth sides of the bin. He could hear them gurgling their last breaths as they sank to the bottom. He was enjoying setting the traps, and had no idea he was being spied on.

* * *

Outside, not far away, Oily Sludge was sheltering from the rain. He had bags under his eyes from nights spent watching the arches, and his neck was still sore from being trapped in his own front door. But like Bennett he was feeling a lot better. His plan was taking shape.

He had some help now. He had enlisted two more cats, the Smacker twins, mercenaries who ranged freely across London and who had bad reputations because of their nasty habits.

The Smackers had no friends, nor did they want any. They were homeless cats who lived by helping themselves to anything they fancied. They were evil by nature and unpleasant to look at. If they had been clean they would have been striped, but they rarely bothered to wash. They could not think of any reason to do it because they spent most of their time in dirty places where a layer of muck provided good camouflage. Their bad habits suited Oily Sludge.

Of course he had to pay them. He had to allow them into his territory, and on top of that he had to act as their guide and let them into some of his best secrets – where, for example, you could get a good smoked haddock or a cooked chicken without much risk.

It was a coincidence that Oily Sludge's idea was a bit like Bennett's. The rats and their monster were to be drowned. What the Smackers planned to do was to use Oily Sludge as a bait to get the Sludge-Gulper to run off the wharf at high tide with them all in it. The Smackers would be safe out of danger one on each side of him. They had watched the old man drive the lorry close to the edge. If they could get Alf still closer and make him lose control, the Sludge-Gulper would splash into the river and sink.

It was a good plan but risky. The Smackers put their price up. They wanted danger money – the freedom of Oily Sludge's territory for ever. It was a high price, but he had to agree. He reckoned he could break the contract afterwards. What he could not agree was who was to do the dangerous bit, who was going to be the one in the middle.

They argued about it, and as they climbed down from the Sludge-Gulper, the three of them were so involved in the plan that they did not notice Totters. He was lying flat on top of the cab, and had heard every word they said.

* * *

It was calm in the arch when Totters got back. Alf was asleep with his cap over his eyes, and the rest of them were relaxing – except for Orse who was on duty at the door. It was as well that he was. The Smackers arrived soon after Totters – as he was filling in the last details of his report.

Orse whistled when he saw them. "Cats . . . Batty . . . Cats . . . real ones . . ."

"Cats . . ." The others joined in.

Alf was out of bed as soon as he heard. He beat his chest, bounced up and down and showed his teeth. It was enough for the Smackers. When they looked over the top of the furniture and saw him they knew that Oily Sludge had a problem. He had told them about an old man, but nothing about a high-jumping hairy monster with teeth. When they saw it they did not waste time talking about it. They disappeared even quicker than they had come.

As they squeezed through the outer door their minds were made up. They knew for sure now who was going to be the one in the middle.

Chapter Twelve

It was high tide with the river almost lapping the top of the wharf, and dark with the moon disappearing at intervals behind clouds. Alf was having a lesson in the Sludge-Gulper, and the Smackers were with Oily Sludge in a crate, watching.

There was not much room in the crate and Oily Sludge was in the middle. The Smackers made sure of that. They were assuring him that there was no risk. They would be on each side ready to help. They would be with him, shining their torches so that he would show up better in the dark. All he had to do was jump sideways at the right moment.

The Sludge-Gulper rattled past, making a convenient smokescreen. "Now . . ." They lifted him up, and as his head came over the top of the crate he saw the tail light. The Sludge-Gulper was turning to come back.

The Smackers kept a firm grip on him as they hurried to the edge of the wharf. They put him in place with his back to the river, and made sure he had his torch. "Hold it under your chin," they reminded him. "Remember . . . when you see us light up, you switch on."

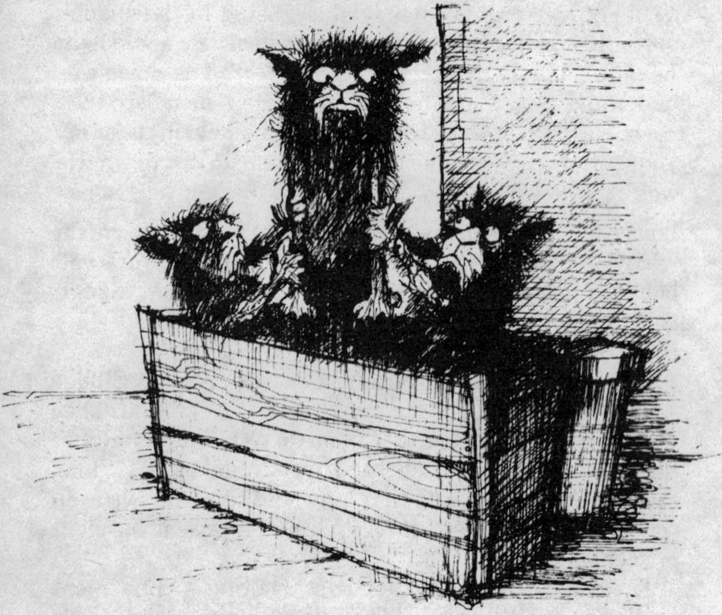

"And don't forget to jump up and down..."

"And make faces..."

"Hold the light under your chin..."

"And make terrible faces..."

"Don't worry... we'll help..."

"We'll be right by you..."

"Shouting..."

Oily Sludge was not happy about being in the middle, but the Sludge-Gulper was on its way back. He could hear the motor thudding – or was it his heart? The noise was louder and closer, and he was lit up. He remembered the torch. He fumbled and switched it on and held it under his chin, and started to make faces and jump up and down. He wanted to shout but his mouth was dry, so he jumped higher and made uglier faces. He knew he was close to the edge, and he wanted to look down and see where he was putting his feet. But it is not easy to look down when you are holding a torch under your chin and pulling faces and jumping all at the same time.

When Alf saw Oily Sludge his reaction was immediate, just as the Smackers had planned. He pulled hard on the steering wheel and the Sludge-Gulper swerved straight for Oily Sludge and the river. The rats also reacted.

"Brake!"

Sid and Orse threw themselves on the handbrake. Batty flicked his tail and switched off the motor. Clappy belted Alf's foot with a specially hard kick so that he slammed it on the brake pedal. The Sludge-Gulper tipped on its nose as though the front wheels had dropped off. But it did not stop. It was carried forward by its own momentum.

Oily Sludge jumped higher. It was working. They were coming straight for him, straight for the river, and they had left it too late to stop. He saw the activity in the cab. They were that close – about to make the big splash. The moment deserved an even uglier face, a goodbye to all of them. He made it, a twisted leer of triumph and revenge, rolling his eye and sticking his tongue out. It was a face so horrible it would stick in their minds as they plunged to the bottom.

Unfortunately he concentrated so hard on making the face that he forgot to jump sideways. He realised this when he was in the air. It had all happened too fast. He was still making the face when he landed on the Sludge-Gulper, right in front of the windscreen.

He looked up and saw what he had secretly been afraid of. It really was a monster, and it was close enough to lean out and grab him. That was bad enough, but there was worse to come.

It was suddenly very quiet, and he felt himself sliding backwards. He heard the splash as he dropped the torch. It would be him next. The Sludge-Gulper tipped slowly towards the river as he clawed for a grip. He stretched every sinew, hoping – almost praying, but it rocked like a see-saw. It was balanced on the wharf with its back wheels in the air and the front ones over the edge. If he slipped off it might tip back and be safe without him. He risked a look down. The water was black. He willed himself away from it towards the cab, but the monster was waiting for him there. He closed his eyes. He knew he was only a claw-tip away from a wet end.

"Smackers . . ." It was a desperate moan, all he could manage. "Smackers . . . where are you? Help . . ."

There was no answer. The Smackers had summed up the situation and were already far enough away to be safe. He was on his own.

Inside the Sludge-Gulper they knew they were close to disaster. The river looked as cold and black to them as it did to Oily Sludge. Batty poked his head out of the window.

"It's all your fault," he shouted. "I hope you slide off and drown."

They were all leaning back instinctively. It was the

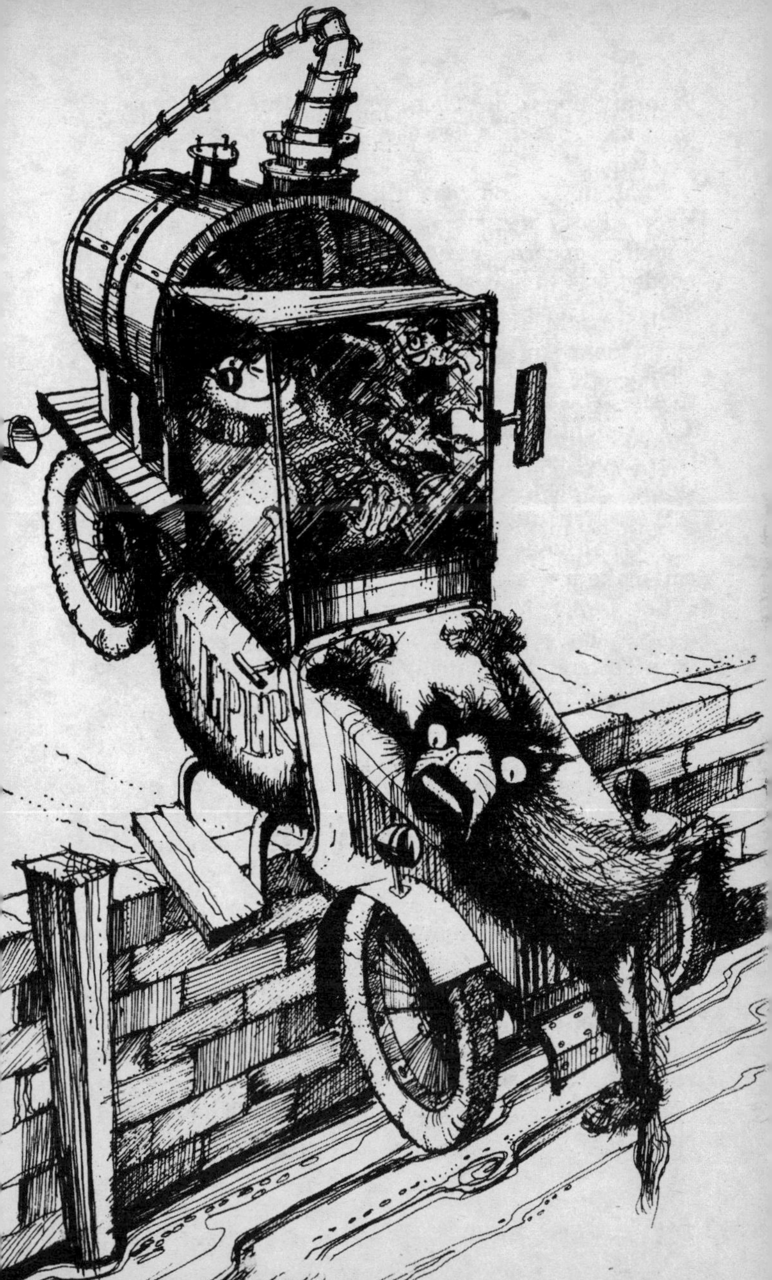

natural thing to do. There was no panic. They were in a tight spot, but they had been in tight spots before.

"Help. . ."

"Shut up . . . and keep still or you'll have us all in the river." Batty was trying to think. His mind raced like jumping popcorn. They only had a few seconds. What they needed was weight at the back to get the wheels on the ground. "Hang on to the brake, Sid . . . and Orse. And Weston . . . take Totters and climb out on the back. We need some weight there." He realised he had to say a word to Alf. "You did all right, Alf." He would have liked to get Alf's weight on the back, but they needed him to drive if they could get the wheels on the ground. "We'll be all right," he said, trying not to look worried.

Weston shouted from outside. He was running along the top of the Sludge-Gulper. "I think we can do it, Batty, if we can make it work."

Batty knew he was clever. "How?"

"It's simple. We'll fill her with river water. I can do it with Totters. But be ready to start the motor. We need it for the pump."

"OK . . . when?"

"Start it now."

Batty was relieved. "Hear that, Clappy?" He switched on and pulled the starter. Clappy pressed the accelerator, and as the motor started Oily Sludge felt it rattle underneath him. It was not a good feeling. He was scared it might shake him off.

With the motor running Weston took over. He had watched the Sludge-Gulper at work many times. "You'll have to help with the pipe, Totters." It was heavy work lifting the flexible hose from its bracket, but the two of them managed to get it free so that they could swing it round and drop the end in the river. Weston stood on the control panel and tried the levers until the hose began to shudder.

"It's sucking, Batty," he shouted. "The pump's working. She's sucking up."

The Sludge-Gulper was doing what it was made for. It sucked noisily – like Alf. "More revs, Clappy." The hose bucked and slurped. "It's sucking a treat. Keep it going." Weston jumped down so that he could see the angle. "More revs . . . give it more revs . . ." The hose thrashed along its length. "Keep it in the river, Totters. Keep the end under water."

They sat in the cab, waiting and willing the idea to work.

"She'll go soon . . ."

Oily Sludge heard and wondered which way. He kept his eyes closed.

"She moved . . . she'll go soon . . ."

They were sitting so still that they felt the slight movement. Weston shouted to Batty. "She's tilting." He stepped back and took a sight along his paw. "Get ready . . . she'll go suddenly. When the back wheels go down, Batty, bang in reverse and make Alf drive. More revs, Clappy."

They were wrapped in a cloud of blue smoke.

"She's going . . . just needs a drop more. Keep the end in the water, Totters. Keep her sucking."

The Sludge-Gulper, almost unexpectedly, slammed down on its back wheels. It went suddenly with a loud bang.

"Reverse . . ."

"Brake off . . ."

"Rev . . . Rev up . . ." Weston screamed.

Batty had all his weight on the gear lever before Alf had time to push down the clutch. The grinding noise was terrible.

"Rev . . ."

The motor roared. The smoke was thicker. It was not a smooth start. It was as though the Sludge-Gulper, given the chance, had decided to jump to safety. It bounced backwards towards the arches dragging the hose which went on gasping for air through the open end.

"Stop . . ." Weston screamed even louder. "Stop . . ."

"Brake . . ." Batty leaped out of the cab. "Keep the pump going," he shouted, "keep it on, Weston."

Oily Sludge risked opening an eye. There was ground below now, where there had been water. He was safe. He opened the other eye and let go.

Batty made a sign and Weston understood. The hose was still bucking as they jumped for it. "Grab him . . ."

As Oily Sludge touched the ground they swung the end of the hose onto him. "More revs . . ."

It was like picking up a rag with a vacuum cleaner. It was lucky for Oily Sludge that he was too large to be sucked into the hose, but he blocked the hole and the suction held him fast. He could not tell whether his feet were on the ground or in the air. He could not jump. He could not walk. He could not run. He was trapped, locked onto the hose. Batty leaned close and shouted.

"Don't ever try anything like that again."

Oily Sludge shook his head.

"Ever . . . do you hear? Ever again. . ."

He was ready to agree to anything and it was a painful sound which came out when he opened his mouth. "No . . ."

It satisfied Batty. "Pump off . . ." The suction stopped and Oily Sludge dropped free. He picked himself up and staggered away. It was the second time they had seen him off, but there was no speed in the way he went this time. He limped away, walking with a sideways tilt in the position he had been fixed to the hose.

If it had not been Oily Sludge, and if he had not looked so funny, they might almost have felt sorry for him.

Chapter Thirteen

"Gentlemen, we're wrong." The zoo Director pointed to a map of the south of England. "We're thinking like humans. That's why we're wrong. We're thinking like humans and we should be trying to think like gorillas." He paused to let the words sink in, and looked thoughtfully down at his feet.

"Here am I in shoes," he tapped them with his pointer, "and clothes – dressed, as we all are, like a human being, and thinking like one. And somewhere out there . . ." he made a sweeping gesture, "somewhere out there is an animal – a wild animal."

He stepped to the window. "Like the other animals we've got in cages – a wild thing without shoes and clothes, a big ape – a naked ape." He came back to the map, stamping his feet to keep their minds on the shoes. There was a photograph of a gorilla by the map, showing the side view of the animal, knuckle walking.

"This," he reminded them, "is what we're looking for. This is our fugitive, and what we seem to have forgotten is that we're not looking for a human fugitive. We're looking for him – a wild one, an entirely different thing."

He touched the picture carefully as he might have done if it had been the gorilla himself. "Just look at him. He's not like one of us, and because we're not thinking like him we're looking in the wrong places." He put a hand to his brow and held it there, as though the act of swelling his forehead made it like the huge brow of a gorilla, and would help him to think like one.

"With a human fugitive," he did not look up, "with a human you have someone whose every instinct would be to get away – as far as possible. Distance means safety. So he would travel as far and as fast as he could. But with an animal," he lowered his voice to a whisper, "the instinct would be different. Those of us who work with animals, who have studied them, know that an escaping animal would not be interested in distance. One mile – a hundred, it wouldn't matter. All that matters to a fleeing animal, a scared creature, is a place to hide."

There was a murmur of agreement.

"And a place to stay hidden – warm if possible, and dry and comfortable, close to food and water." He pointed to the map again. "We've been on the wrong track entirely."

With the help of an assistant he pinned up a new map. It was a map of London with the zoo marked in red. "I think," he stressed the I, "I think our gorilla is somewhere here, still in London, probably close to us. Perhaps . . ." he looked out of the window again, "perhaps even here, hiding in the zoo somewhere."

There was a buzz of interest among the audience, and many questions.

"How far could a gorilla travel?"

"Would it move by day or night?"

"Could he be sure the gorilla was still in London?"

Not positively sure, he had to admit. But he had given it a lot of thought. What he could be sure of was that their search, although it was well organised and costly, had failed for the simple reason that they had not been thinking like a gorilla. He asked them to put themselves in the same situation. What would they do? How would they behave if they were escaped gorillas?

He would tell them. They would not take a train or bus out to the country – or even make for it on foot. Gorillas do not know that London is surrounded by country. What a gorilla would look for would be an open place. London was where they had to search – in all the open places.

The gorilla, he went on, is a forest dweller, and an escaped one would look for a place with trees and bushes where he could build a nest and hide. London had lots of parks. That's where he would be – in one of the parks. All they had to do was search them.

The message went out to all the parks – from the high class royal parks with lots of space to the smallest playground in the suburbs. When they got the message the keepers took on a new role. They were no longer there just to keep an eye on things. Now they were hunters looking for tracks, and in particular for tracks of the big feet of a gorilla.

In Battersea park, a few minutes walk from the arches, the keepers began searching at once. They looked under all the bushes and studied the soft earth of the flower beds. They even searched along the foreshore of the river which ran the length of the park, but there were no signs in the mud of bare feet or of knuckles. The Director had insisted on including this important detail in the message. The gorilla had the habit of knuckle walking, using the middle joint of his clenched fingers to lean on.

The keepers in Battersea park were conscientious but they were looking so hard for signs of a bare-footed knuckle walking gorilla that they passed close to Alf without seeing him. Nor did they see Sid and Clappy fishing in the goldfish pond.

The old man sitting on the bench by the pond, looking after a baby, was a common sight in the park. There were always people with children there. And they could not be expected to know that instead of a baby in the pram there was a plastic bowl with goldfish swimming in it.

Sid and Clappy were trawling for them. They had a bit of net curtain with strings tied at the corners and they were dragging it across the pond. At the right moment, just as they got close enough to Alf, they flicked the net over their heads. The goldfish hardly had time to notice before they were out of the pond and in the plastic bowl.

When they had enough Alf pushed the pram out of the park and back to the arches.

* * *

Bennett came back early. They could see he was cheerful. Before coming in he looked through a crack in the door and saw that the plan had worked. He remembered exactly how he had left the traps, with the apples still and covering the surface of each bin. Now there were gaps and the apples were bobbing about. There were even some spilled on the floor.

Dead! He rubbed his hands together. Drowned! All of them! Dead at last!

The door scraped noisily as he let himself in but he did

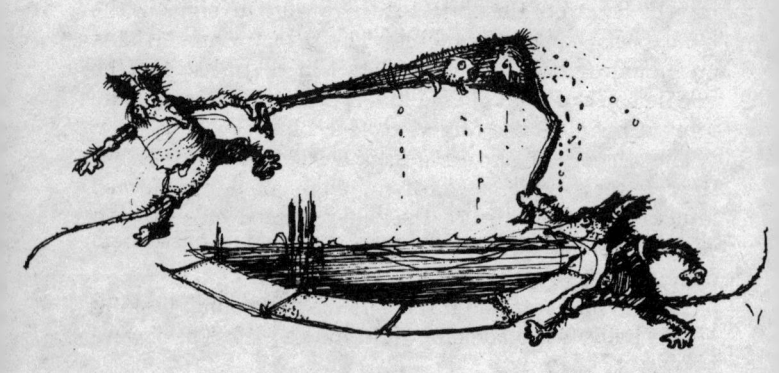

not bother to lift it. There was no one to hear. When he stepped inside he could hardly believe what he saw. All the traps had caught rats. There were gaps on the surface of every bin.

"At last . . ." He was unusually quiet. It was a solemn moment but he felt no pity for the rats. They had been robbing him for as long as he could remember. It had been a long struggle but he had won in the end. He always knew he would. Rats were only animals. People were cleverer.

He was smiling as he chose the nearest trap and divided the floating apples. He was so excited his hands shook and he splashed water on his trousers, but he did not care. It was there – the first drowned rat – dead, with its eyes wide open.

It looked up at him and blinked, slowly opening and closing its mouth. For a moment, as the water settled, Bennett was afraid the rat was still alive and gasping for breath. Then as the eyes became part of a shape he saw it was the wrong colour. The smile vanished. Bennett took off his hat, threw it on the water and beat his head with his fist.

"Fish! Fish! They've put fish in my traps. Rats in the fish traps," he shouted. "No, I mean fish in the rat traps." He was confused. "Look at me . . ." he stretched out his arms, "look at me . . . hard working . . . honest . . . and what do I get? I lose my fruit and I get fish . . ." He went to each of the traps in turn but already knew what he would find. He kicked each bin, startling the goldfish.

Totters, watching with the others could not help whispering. "Look at him. He's unique. The only human who goes fishing with rat-traps."

Batty silenced him with a flick of his tail. They had scored a victory, but he doubted if the problem of Bennett was over yet.

"Fish . . . rats . . . fish . . . rats . . ." Bennett was sobbing as he staggered out to the wharf. The rats waited, and

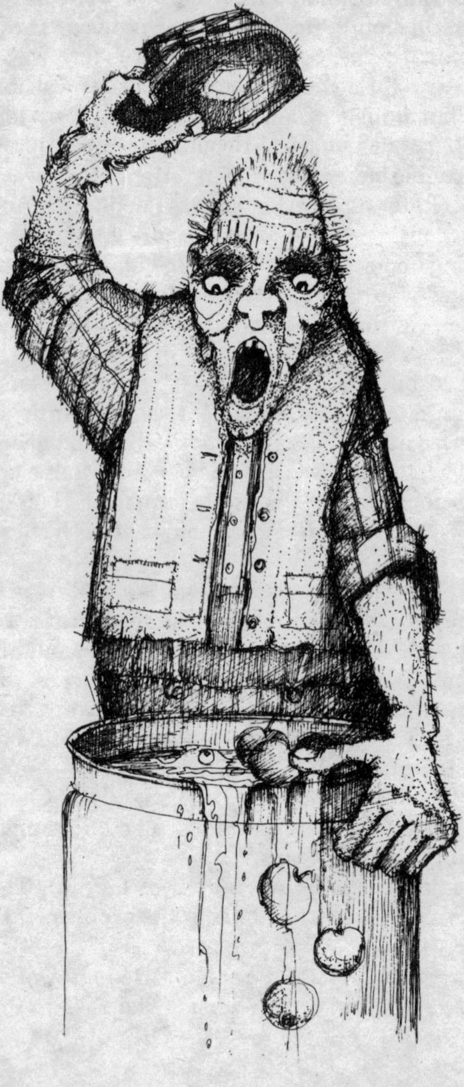

when it was safe they followed Sid. They jumped from their hiding place and pushed the bins over so that the goldfish spilled onto the floor. It was not easy picking up the flapping fish, especially since there were wet apples rolling around, but they collected them carefully, seeing who could catch the most – and ran with them onto the wharf, where they dropped them gently into the river.

Chapter Fourteen

On Sunday they took Alf to church. He set fire to the belfry.

Batty liked them all to dress up on Sundays and go to morning service, though at breakfast, when they talked about the problem of getting Alf in, it seemed that they might have to change their routine. As rats they could slip in unnoticed, but at church most of the congregation knew each other, and the vicar talked to all of them. It would be diffficult for Alf, but Batty insisted they had to work something out for him. They had a minder so they could do more things, not less.

In the end they settled for the belfry. There was a gallery a few steps up from the organ, and from it he would be able to see down into the church.

They arrived early and Alf stood for a moment sniffing the unusual scents. It was a new place but he liked it. The sun, streaming through the windows, was making coloured patterns on the floor, and there were lots of shiny things. They hurried him through the organ loft up to the next level.

The service started and they settled down to join in. They knew some of the words and made up the others, and sang extra loud because they were so near the organ. Alf watched and moved his lips like them, and found himself making sounds he had never made before.

He was not sure what he had to do when they put their paws together and closed their eyes. When he tried it nothing happened. He just felt sleepy.

It might have been the incense or the candles, but it was during prayers that he sniffed the smoke and decided to join in. He slipped the stolen cigarette box and matches from his pocket. The cigarette wobbled in his lips and he made the end soggy, and he had to try several times before he managed to light it. But he had seen lots of people do it when he was in the zoo, and when he sorted out the difference between puffing and blowing he got it going.

He coughed a bit, which made Sid open an eye. "You're smoking, Alf!" He sounded surprised.

Alf nodded. He coughed again and took another puff.

"Alf's smoking." Sid nudged Batty in the middle of the prayer.

Batty sniffed hard as he opened his eyes. He waved his arms to clear the smoke. "Not in church, Alf." He looked anxiously down at the vicar. "You can't smoke."

Alf puffed harder.

"It's not allowed." Batty jumped onto his knee and made urgent signs. "You'll be found out. Get rid of it."

Alf seemed to understand. He lifted Batty from his knee and got up.

"Hymn number 542 . . ."

The organ started. They were safe. No one had noticed. Batty gave Alf an approving nod as he came back to his chair without the cigarette. The belfry shook as the organist put on full power, and they joined in.

"From victory unto victory . . .
His army he shall lead . . .

Till every foe is vanquished . . ."
They thought about Bennett and Oily Sludge.
"The trumpet call obey . . .
When duty calls or danger . . ."

It was then that they discovered the belfry was on fire. For years it had been used to store old hymn books and hassocks and chairs with cane seats. The hassocks had been nibbled by mice and were spilling out sawdust, and when Alf dropped his cigarette it began to smoulder. There was a draught which started a flame, then a fire which quickly began to spread.

The rats beat the flames with hymn books. They went at it bravely, jumping about so that they would not get singed. But the sawdust was dry and they were fanning the flames as much as putting them out. Sid saw they were in serious trouble. They needed water or fire-extinguishers. It was a job for the firemen.

From then on it all happened quickly. "Fire . . ." The vicar was in the pulpit, looking up. "Fire . . ." He spread his arms wide. The congregation were used to the vicar's sermons. He often started by surprising them. "Fire . . ." He pointed upwards. "The church is on fire."

When they began to smell the smoke they believed him. The church was empty in seconds. Alf and the rats had already left. As they steered him round the corner the first fire-engine was on its way. He wanted to stop and watch, but Batty hurried him on. He was pleased to see the fire-engine himself, but this was the moment to put as much distance as possible between themselves and the fire.

Chapter Fifteen

Sunday night was bath night. There were a number of houses the rats used. They liked a soak in hot water at least once a week, and one of their favourite bathrooms was in a house not far away, where the water was always hot and there were plenty of clean towels.

They had no trouble with Alf in the streets now. He walked upright nearly all the time and was ready to go anywhere with them. They took him past the church on the way to the house and were all relieved to see there was no sign of any damage. The lights were on for the evening service and they could hear the organ.

Sid and Clappy were waiting for them with the door open. It was a good house. They knew there would be plenty of food in the kitchen, and the bathroom was luxurious with mirrors all round the walls. They also knew the house was always empty on Sundays.

Alf needed a bath. He had not had one since they got him, and after the fire he smelt badly of smoke. When they took him upstairs Weston had the bath ready, steaming and covered with bubbles. He was testing the temperature with the tip of his tail as they came in.

When Alf saw his reflection in the mirrors he looked fierce and showed his teeth. The reflections showed theirs, and when he beat his chest they did the same. Totters understood. He jumped on the side of the bath and pointed to himself and then at all the other Totters. "It's me," he said, "and they're all me. They're pictures of me – and those are all you, Alf." He waited, not sure what Alf would do.

"It's a bath. You have to get in it." Batty jumped up with him and pointed at the bubbles. "It's ready for you. It's your bath night. You'll like it."

Alf was not sure.

"You'll really like it."

When he did not move Batty saw it was the moment for another lesson. "Don't worry, Alf," he smiled. "A bath is for getting in – like this." As he spoke he gave Totters a push. "See, Alf. You get in like Totters. It's easy."

Totters came to the surface spluttering. He blew out a stream of bubbles, and floated on his back with his head out of the water. "It's smashing, Alf," he laughed. "Come in. It's warm."

Alf made up his mind. He stepped to the bath, climbed on the side and jumped. It was like a depth-charge. Alf displaced almost half the water. It hit the ceiling and slapped across the room, soaking them all. It was wet and noisy, and he loved it. As the bubbles slid down the mirrors he beat his hands on what was left, making more splashes.

Batty had been swept over by a miniature tidal wave and was on his back on the floor with his feet in the air. Totters was somewhere under the bubbles. The rest of them were sliding about, wiping their eyes and laughing as they tried to stand up.

Alf was laughing too. He cupped water in his hands and threw it at them. Remembering what Totters had done he sucked up bubbles and blew them out in a stream.

"He's still got his hat on!" Weston was shocked. "And

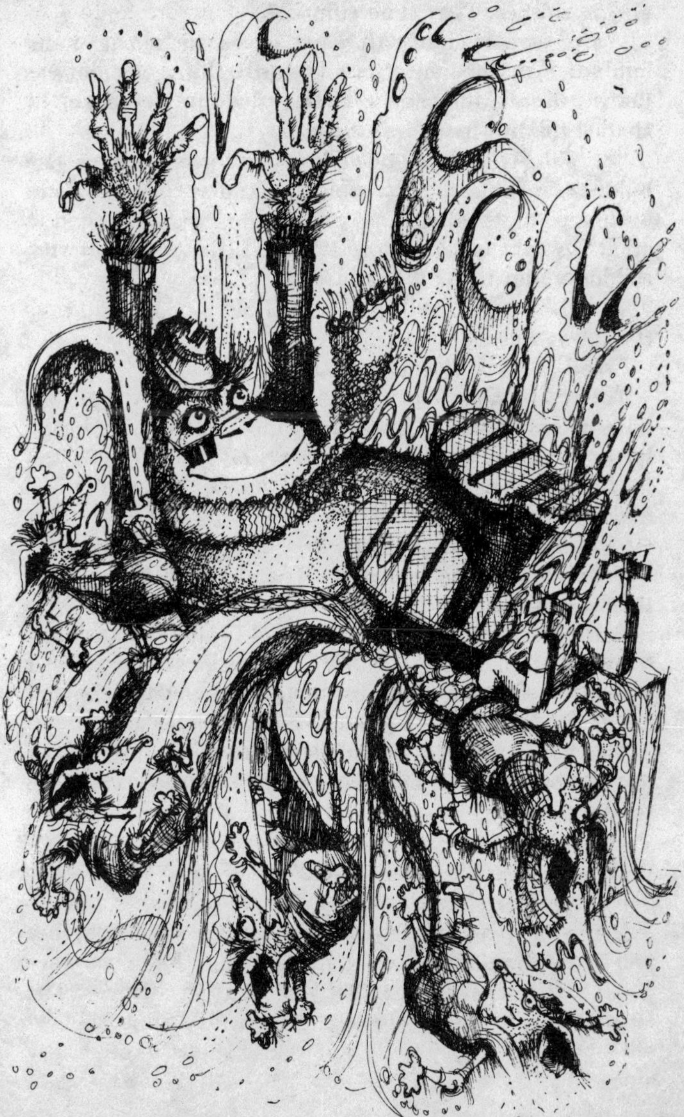

all his clothes. They'll be ruined."

Water streamed off Alf's hat as he sucked up more bubbles. For a moment they could do nothing. His aim was getting better, and they were busy dodging the jets as he shaped his lips for more pressure.

"Stop it, Alf!" Batty tried to sound serious, but he had bubbles on the end of his nose. "You don't get in a bath with your clothes on. That's the wrong way." He had to duck. "A bath is for getting clean in." He looked around, suddenly alarmed. "Where's Totters?"

Totters' head poked up. He was holding Alf's collar as though it was a life-raft. "I'm here."

"Well get out. It's Alf's bath."

Totters climbed onto the side and shook himself. He looked sadly down at his own clothes. "You pushed me," he complained, "with my clothes on, my Sunday clothes."

"In the cause of duty," Batty shrugged, "had to do it . . . had to give him a lesson."

"I was under him. I could have drowned. He's heavy."

They calmed the younger rat, and began to organise themselves for clearing up. They had to show Alf how people have a bath. The overcoat had shrunk and they had to pull together to get it off. They had another shower when they dragged off his boots. It was a wet and slippery business, and then they had to start all over again.

They showed him how to fill the bath and test the water for himself. When it was ready and he lowered himself in they showed him how to scrub himself all over and use the shampoo without getting it in his eyes.

Totters and Clappy helped Weston drag his clothes downstairs for spin-drying, while Sid and Orse stayed to rub him down with warm towels. They worked together and by the time they had finished Alf and the house were clean and fairly dry, and Alf was tingling all over. The only problem was his clothes. Weston had done his best with them, but they were not really smart enough any more.

Chapter Sixteen

Monday evening they were in the shopping centre at Clapham Junction. The shops were closed but they were shopping. Clappy and Orse had just let them into a men's outfitter.

They found a new overcoat for Alf. He chose it himself, a grey one with a smooth lining and a rough outside which he found good to stroke. He put it on over the blue one.

They had problems with other clothes for him. They could not find a shirt with arms long enough nor could they get shoes big enough, and in the end they had to put his boots back on. Size was the problem. Although they were getting him to behave like a human, Weston was finding it difficult to dress him like one.

There were lots of shops and the outing was going so well that Batty let his guard slip for a moment and disaster struck.

Batty stayed with Alf while the others were scouting ahead, and while they were waiting outside a shop he was distracted by what he saw next door. It was a jewellers with trays of watches in the window. Batty needed one badly since he had given his own to Alf. And Alf needed a new one since he had dipped the other one in the celery bath.

While they waited Batty saw something interesting. The shop windows were all covered with a strong grille but there was a letter-box low down in the front door. It would only take a second. He made sure they were alone, jumped down and wriggled through the letter-box. He chose good watches with gold bracelets and slipped back the way he had come. But when he came out he could not believe it. Alf was not there.

When Sid heard Batty whistle he came at once and found him hopping about in agitation. He saw immediately what was up. "Where is he, Batty? Where's Alf?"

"He was here, right here on the pavement. I only left him for a second..."

The others arrived as he spoke.

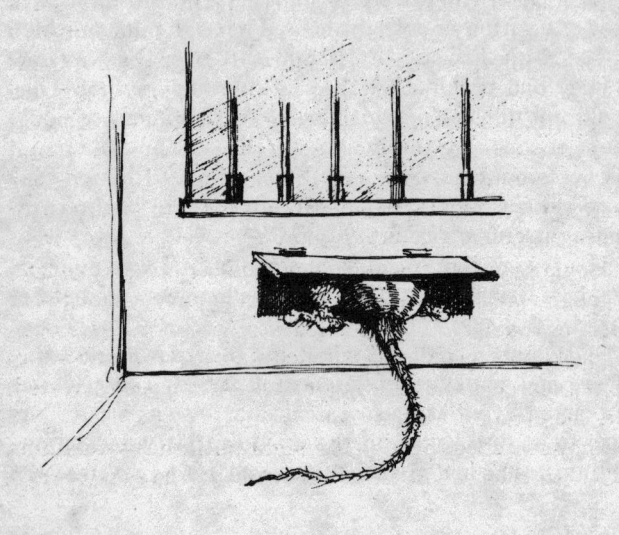

"He was here..." Batty pointed to the pavement, "on this spot. And then he was gone – vanished." He looked up at the building as though he expected Alf might be climbing it. "I don't understand, Sid. I left him here."

"And where were you?" Sid frowned.

Batty held out the watches. "Shopping . . . for him and me. I went in there and got 'em . . . and came straight out, but he wasn't here."

"Something scared him." Sid patted Batty's shoulder. "He's hiding. He won't be far away." He made a sign to the others. "Don't worry . . . we'll find him."

Batty waited while the others searched. The minutes ticked by on the new watches.

* * *

"He must be around somewhere." Totters looked out for the tenth time. "He can't just disappear. A gorilla can't disappear in the middle of Clapham Junction. It's not possible."

"Keep still, Totters." Batty wanted to think. They had moved round the corner, away from the main road, and were holding an emergency meeting in the back of a lorry. "A gorilla can't disappear . . . you're right. But Alf's not a gorilla now, is he? He's more like a human. You'll have to go out again and look at all the people. Send 'em out again, Sid, and make sure they look everywhere and at everyone, especially anybody in a grey coat."

The second search was also a failure. As evening became night and the streets grew quieter they ranged all over the district. They looked over every fence and went into gardens and yards. They climbed trees and ran through empty buildings. They hardly gave a thought to their own safety. They looked at everybody. Orse even slipped into Lavender Hill police-station. He found a way in and searched the building in case Alf had been arrested, but the cells were empty.

They searched through the night until the street lights switched themselves off and dawn began to take over. It was a grey dawn for all of them, especially Batty, but it was light and there was no sign of Alf, and they had to go home without him. They were sad. The bed was ready. There was fruit on the table and the armchair was empty.

When Bennett arrived next door and started shouting it was too much. Totters hammered on the wall and shouted back. "Shut up! Shut up you miserable old devil!"

Batty hushed him at once, but he was not angry with him. He knew how Totters felt. They all felt the same. "Not now, Totters . . ." He carefully pulled him back from the wall. "We'll see to Bennett later. We'll shut him up for good . . . but not now." He would have liked to shout himself. Shouting might have made them all feel better, but he had to keep things under control. They had lost their minder, and if they did not stay calm they could be in worse trouble. He gripped Totters' arm and pointed to the wall. Totters understood and stopped shouting – but it was too late.

Bennett looked at the wall. The noise had come from the other side. But there was no one there. It was just a store for junk and old furniture. Nobody lived there. Or did they? He had heard something, and the more he thought about it the more certain he became. A store piled high with junk was a perfect place for someone to hide. That was why he was losing so much fruit. It was not just rats. There was someone else thieving. Someone had moved in next door.

He rubbed his stubbly chin and smiled. The discovery made him feel a lot better.

Chapter Seventeen

Alf was in Chelsea, the other side of the river from Battersea. It happened quickly when they were shopping and the others went on ahead. He felt Batty slip out of the scarf, and it was when he was by himself that the bus stopped. The conductor, seeing the old man with bad eyesight waiting at the bus-stop, stepped down and insisted on helping him onto the bus and to a seat.

Alf was confused when the bus started but he recognised the noise and settled down. He enjoyed riding past all the lights, and after a while when people near him got up from their seats he did the same. He followed them onto the pavement and let himself drift along with the crowd.

Sometimes he stood still and looked in a shop window. He touched the glass carefully. There were lots of things he would have liked but he knew that the glass must be there to stop him taking them.

There were so many things to see, but later when he was hungry, he remembered his friends and did what they would have done. He followed his nose to somewhere which smelt promising and, making sure he was alone, lifted himself over a wall.

He found himself in a place stacked with boxes, and stepped past them to a door. He leaned on it until it opened, took a deep sniff and smiled. It was the right sort of smell. He took a quick look round and helped himself to a bunch of bananas.

When he climbed back over the wall he moved away from the bright lights. He found a place with trees where he could sit down. He chose a bench in the darkest corner. It was good because his feet were aching. He could have sat there happily but something was troubling him. He was not sure what to do next. He wanted to be still, perhaps to sleep a little, but he kept thinking about his friends. They never sat still when they were out. They were always running about and searching, and finding new things. He was beginning to miss them.

If they had been with him they would have told him what to do. He yawned and closed his eyes. He ought to go, but it would be good to sleep for a while.

It was not long before the policeman found him. The footsteps separated themselves from the background noises and Alf was instantly alert. He had an eye open and sat very still, not sure what was going to happen.

"You all right, sir?" The man had shiny buttons and a hat like his own, the one he wore in bed. "You're not ill are you, sir?"

Alf nodded, keeping his nose well down in the scarf.

"Don't you think you should be getting home, sir? It's late to be sitting outside."

The man was coming too close. Alf wanted to be by himself. If he reached out he could pick him up – or just give him a push. He would not have to push hard. He could do it with one hand. Then he would be alone again, but he had the feeling that the man was a friend.

He stood waiting. Alf had to do something. He crouched low and took a deep breath. He took a hand from his pocket and felt along the bench till he had a good grip. He used it to push himself suddenly upright so that, when he was on his feet, he could twist round towards the dark.

The policeman was taken by surprise as Alf sprang off the bench and shambled away. It was late for anyone to be sitting in the gardens on a cold night, especially an old man wearing dark glasses. Perhaps he had bad eyes and nowhere to go. It would be unkind to disturb him. He seemed harmless but the policeman was not sure. There was something odd about the old man, something about his shape and the way he walked.

"Excuse me, sir . . ." He went after him. "Just a minute, sir."

Alf heard the shout. He looked over his shoulder, slapped a hand on his hat and took off at speed.

When the policeman reached the road there was no sign of the old man. He stood listening, slightly out of breath, trying to make up his mind. Across the road there were high railings. The old man could not have climbed them. The policeman was not sure he could have climbed them himself. But there was nobody in sight. There was only one thing to do. He used his radio to call for help.

Fortunately for Alf who was up a tree on the other side of the railings they laughed at the police-station when they got the message. A young policeman ought to be able to catch an old man without help, even one acting suspiciously. They told him to get on with it, so he shrugged his shoulders and went back to his beat.

Alf watched him go. He was smiling. The high bars had not stopped him. He had just pulled himself up hand over hand, and dropped down on the other side – and then climbed the nearest tree. He felt safe up there. It was dark and good for hiding in. He rubbed his fingers and touched the branch where he was sitting. It was rough and felt right.

Later, when he was sure he was alone, he climbed down and set off through the trees away from the road. He knew he was going the right way because of the smell. It was unmistakable.

There were high bars again. He looked through them. There was a road, and on the other side a low wall. He was careful and pulled himself up into another tree so that he could see better. It was there, exactly as he wanted it to be – the water with lights shining in it. It had its own special smell and as soon as he saw it he knew he was nearly home.

It was safe in the tree but he did not stay. He dropped down, climbed the bars and crossed the road. He leaned on the wall and took deep breaths. The water was close. He could almost touch it. It was moving fast and it was a long way to the other side, but over there – that was where he would find his friends. All he had to do was get across to them, and there was a way. If he looked sideways he could see lights in a straight line crossing to the other side. It was the way home.

Suddenly he felt a tap on his shoulder. He had heard nothing. He had been thinking hard about his friends. He turned, startled but ready.

"You got a light, mate?"

It was a man, a small man. Alf recognised the cigarette he held out and reached into his pocket for matches.

"Thanks, mate."

As the match flared Alf saw the face in detail. It was thin. He could have covered it easily with his hand, and it had glasses, just like he did.

"You by yourself?"

Alf nodded.

"Me too," the man shivered, "cold ain't it?"

Alf decided he was friendly.

"Got nowhere to stay then?"

Alf nodded.

"Me neither." The cigarette glowed. "Well I have now, a sort of place. You want to see it? You want a cup of tea? I could make us one. It's not far, only along there. Come on, I'll show you."

Alf felt a gentle pressure on his arm, pulling him away from the wall. As he was led along he saw he could look down on the man. He could have picked him up.

The man went on talking. "I was like you . . . homeless, nowhere to go. But I found a place for the winter." He shivered again. "It gets cold in winter, don't it?"

It was not far. When they stopped the man let go of his arm, then surprised him by climbing over a gate. "It's locked," he whispered. "Can you manage it?" He turned to help Alf and nodded approvingly when he lifted himself over. "Follow me." He walked carefully across a plank with water running under it. "This way." He bent down and lifted a flap. "Down here. Mind the step. It's dark. And shut it after you."

Alf felt his way down. He stood for a moment at the bottom until he could see.

"I said, shut it." The man stepped past him and closed the flap. When he came back he lit a candle. Alf saw that it was a place to live in, a small place with a bed and another one above it.

"It's a bit cold and damp. Boats are always damp. It ain't been lived in for a long time so I'm staying for the winter – squatting." He chuckled. "It's not much but it's better than nothing. Go on then . . . sit down." He pointed to the bed.

Alf stepped carefully across the cluttered floor.

"It ain't tidy, but don't worry. Sit on the bottom bunk. Make yourself at home. I'll get some tea." While he busied himself he spoke over his shoulder. "What d'you think of it? Ain't bad is it? I'm making the place comfortable for the winter."

Alf tried hard to understand.

"Here's your tea. Drink it while it's hot."

Alf took the cup with both hands, trying not to spill it. It was hot, hot enough to hurt, and when he tried it with the tip of his tongue it was not a nice taste.

"I ain't got no sugar, I'm afraid, nor anything to eat."

Eat – Alf knew the word, and he remembered the bananas. He put the cup down and picked up his shopping bag.

"What's in there?" The man watched him. "Bananas! Funny thing to have," he said, but he seemed pleased. "I ain't had a banana for years." He peered at Alf. "You don't say much, do you? Can't you talk?"

Alf nodded.

"Great!" The man shook his head. "We make a great pair. I get myself some company and it turns out you can't talk. You can't talk and I can't see much. We'll get on all right."

They ate and drank together, tea and bananas. Alf sat on the bunk, and the man cleared himself a space on the floor. "You like bananas, don't you. You really like them."

Alf smiled.

"And I like you." The man got up and broke off another banana. "I like your coat too." It's a good coat, thick and warm." He rubbed the material between his fingers. "Not like mine. Mine's worn out. Look at it." He pulled a thread from a frayed cuff. "I'd like a coat like that for the winter, lovely wool like that. I had a new coat once – a long time ago."

He patted Alf's sleeve and smiled at him. Then wrapping his own thin coat tightly round himself he climbed to the top bunk. He went on talking and Alf listened. The man laughed a lot, but gradually his voice got fainter and fainter.

When Alf woke he saw it was day. There were chinks of light coming through cracks in the walls, and a ray of sunlight through a hole in the roof. It shone on the steps and he remembered where he was. It was time to go. He lowered himself without a sound from the bunk and looked at the figure huddled on the one above. He was still sleeping.

As Alf was about to leave he stopped at the steps and turned back. He hesitated for a moment, careful not to make any noise. Then he took off his new coat, stepped back and lifted it gently onto the sleeping figure.

He paused at the top of the steps to make sure it was safe. He took a deep breath of morning air. The water still smelt good. He closed the flap silently, and when he was sure there was nobody near he stepped across the plank to the gate.

When he stood upright on the pavement he wanted to get across the water and go straight home, but he had something to do first. He pulled his hat on tight, took a firm grip of the shopping bag and turned away from the bridge and from his friends on the other side.

Chapter Eighteen

Batty sat in Alf's chair. He was tired and dejected. His eyes were sore and he knew he was making them worse by rubbing them. He had a bad feeling that they had lost Alf for ever – and it was his fault. He should have been more careful. He was in charge. He would have expected it of the others. He should have made a strict rule from the beginning – always one of them with Alf whenever they went out. He was not ready to be by himself in London.

It was a sad morning. Sid came back with the first report – negative. He had searched the Junction shops and the market. Totters had worked with him and they were both dusty and out of breath. "Nothing . . . not a sign of him."

"He's not up the Junction . . . nowhere." Totters yawned and stretched. "We looked everywhere. There are plenty of people about now – some of them just like him, but not Alf. He's not there."

"You're sure you looked everywhere?"

"Everywhere, Batty, even where he could be hiding if he wanted to stay out of sight. From here to the Junction and back, we looked everywhere, didn't we, Sid?"

Sid nodded and settled wearily on the chair close to Batty. The report from Orse and Weston was the same. No luck. They tried all the places Alf knew, including the church and supermarket and the park. They had been chased out of the church by a cleaner and out of the supermarket by the manager. They had ranged all over the park and along the river, and had not stopped running since they left. They were exhausted.

Clappy arrived back last. His job had been the most difficult. He had searched the circus. He went by himself because one rat could slip in and out of a cage quicker than two. It was risky and the animals made a fuss.

The elephants, each of them chained by a hind leg, knew he was there the moment he was in their tent. They stamped and trumpeted and made so much noise that their trainer came running, but Clappy had gone before he arrived. He searched every part of the circus, even looked up at the trapezes in the big top, but there was no sign of Alf.

Weston lay with his head on his paws and looked at the ticket.

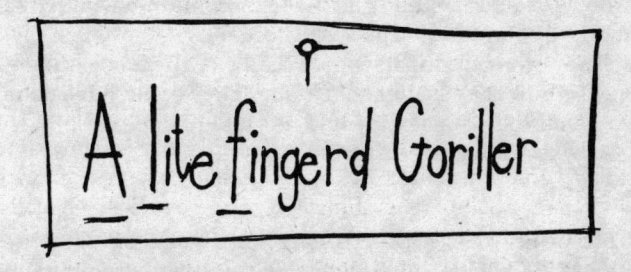

> A lite fingerd Goriller

He read it out softly. It had been unkind to call Alf that, even though it was a little bit true.

Sid and Batty dozed in the armchair. They had been together so long that each knew what the other was thinking. Sid understood that Batty was sad and angry with himself, and Batty knew that Sid was feeling sorry for him and even more sorry about Alf.

It was the saddest day they could remember. They usually had plenty to say when they were together, but now they just wanted to be quiet. They were beginning to realise how much they had grown to like Alf. They would miss feeling safe because he was with them, but it was not just losing their minder which made them sad. They could find a way of getting another one, although a gorilla was probably out of the question. It was more than a minder. Alf was special. He was not the most handsome human – they had to admit that. But he was fun. He enjoyed everything and always tried to do his best when they helped him. They remembered how he was patient and always ready to smile, and although he had some bad habits, they were not his fault. He was still learning.

As the morning dragged on they talked occasionally. Perhaps he was back in the zoo, in a cage. They would go to see him if he was, and take him presents. They wondered if he was still free. Perhaps he would be lucky and find new friends to look after him, children perhaps, who would understand and hide him. Children would like him. They would not be scared of him.

They wondered if he would think of them sometimes, and of how they had changed him. They could have done so much together if they had not lost him.

It was a long, sad morning.

* * *

Totters heard it first. His ears were younger than the others. "Psssttt . . ." He whistled the usual warning and all their ears flicked up. "Someone coming . . ."

Suddenly they were no longer weary. They were tense, listening, with every muscle ready. The steps came closer. Bennett? Not at this time in the morning. Closer . . .

Batty pointed and Sid slipped down to the floor and

crept to the barricade. The others watched him climb to the top and flatten himself, with his tail hanging down on their side.

The steps came nearer. When they stopped outside, Sid flicked his tail once – first warning. When he saw a finger at the door he flicked again – danger. Then as a hand appeared he gave the action signal, a double flick. The others were immediately out of sight. He felt a slight vibration at his side and knew it was Batty. When he took a quick look down into the arch it was empty, except for the furniture.

The door scraped on the ground. They kept the hinges specially loose. It was the danger moment. Sid and Batty did not move nor did they take their eyes off the door. Whoever was coming was being very careful. The door opened slowly. Then they saw him.

"Alf!" They shouted together. "Alf!"

He looked up with a big smile, and Batty and Sid were flying through the air even before he was inside. Sid shouted as he jumped. "It's Alf! He's back!"

Batty landed on Alf's shoulder and hugged him, or as much of him as his arms would go round. "You're back, Alf! You're safe . . . you're back . . ."

By the time he was inside they had all jumped on him. The moment they heard the news they were over the furniture and leaping into space, with tails trailing – all of them shouting.

"Alf . . ."
"Alf . . ."
"Alf . . ."

They landed on his shoulders and hung on, hugging him. Orse even jumped up and down on his hat, clapping and cheering. "Alf, dear old Alf, you're home . . . you're home . . ."

They scrambled to get the best position on him. And Alf in turn held them gently in his great arms, happy to let them run over him. He was home and they were waiting for him. They had not forgotten him.

It was a magic moment. He started to climb the barricade without waiting to be told. He climbed easily. Nothing had changed – except that he had been by himself with lots of other people, and had managed it alone and found his way back with presents for all of them. He held his shopping bag with special care as he rolled over and dropped onto the mattresses.

Chapter Nineteen

An old man with a white face, very wrinkled, and with long hair, he was right, there was someone living next door.

Bennett was unloading potatoes when he happened to look up and notice a brick slightly out of place high up on the wall. A brick out of place in a wall is not special, but it is if you are suspicious.

He piled the sacks against the wall and climbed up to the brick, and saw at once that it had been fixed. It had been scraped clean so that it would move easily, and the one on the other side was the same.

He climbed down, got his barrow ready and did what he always did. He shouted and banged and made a lot of noise dragging the barrow out. He pushed it along the wharf and out of the gate, but that was as far as he went. Instead of going to the market he left it there and came back – silently.

When he was inside he tip-toed to the sacks and climbed again. His hand was shaking as he moved the bricks until he had a gap large enough to see through. When he put his eye to it he looked straight down at an old man with a white face.

It was an accident that made Alf white. When the hugging and welcome were over and he was settled in his chair he gave out his presents. He had something for each of them, and it was the one he gave Totters which caused the accident.

It was a shiny box with gold edges. Alf had picked it out because it was beautiful. Totters opened it and when he saw what was inside he put the tip of his nose in and sniffed. It was talcum powder, and Totters passed it round so they could all have a sniff. When they passed it to Alf he did not quite get it right. Instead of sniffing he blew. The powder exploded in a cloud and when it settled Alf had changed colour. He was white. It made them all laugh so he did it again, blowing harder, and became whiter. It made him laugh too.

That was when Bennett put his eye to the gap. He was right. There was someone next door, a squatter or even someone hiding from the police. It was a surprise but he kept calm. He had to work it out. He risked another look. The old man was laughing. So was Bennett as he climbed quietly down.

* * *

"It's a great disguise – better than anything we've thought of." They were talking about Alf's new look.

"Terrific! They'll never catch him now he's changed colour, now he's white." Batty had laughed as much as the others but he was more serious now. The accident might have been a stroke of luck.

"It makes him look right dignified," said Orse.

"And important. Pity we didn't think of it before." Weston was beating the powder out of Alf's hat. "He's more human now – almost perfect, with the dark rings under his eyes and the wrinkles. You look good, Alf, real good."

Alf gave him a big smile.

"Except for your teeth. They're a bit too healthy. You'd better not show them so much. Old men don't have teeth like yours." Weston cleaned the sunglasses and led Alf to the mirror. He liked what he saw.

"Perfect!" Batty was very happy. "We can take him anywhere now. Anywhere, Alf . . . understand?"

"His coat!" They had not noticed it in the excitement, but Weston was about to brush it. "Look at his coat, Batty. He's lost his new one, the grey one. What have you done with it, Alf?"

Alf smiled.

"He's put it down somewhere, probably forgotten it – expect it was too hot over his fur," suggested Totters.

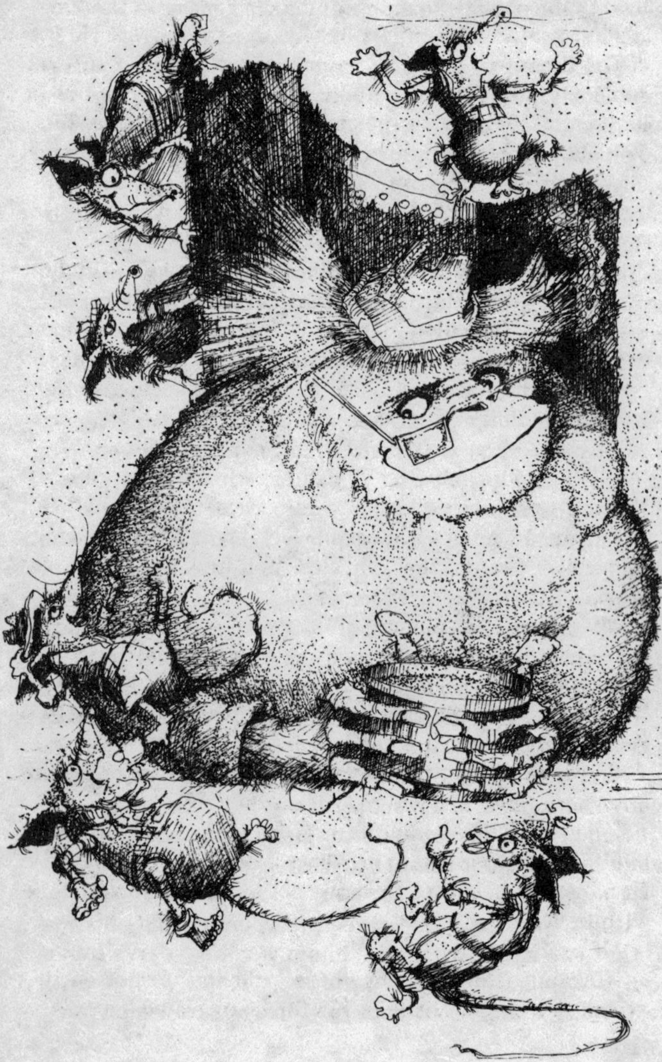

Weston shook his head. "Pity – a grey coat wouldn't show up the powder so much. It makes a mess on the blue one."

"You'll have to brush it – powder him before he puts it on." Batty was thinking about how they could use the accident.

"Or we can get another one from the same shop."

"Not a chance, Totters." Batty was firm. He was still recovering from their last trip. He looked at his watch. "He'll be hungry, Sid. Nip next door for him."

Sid and Clappy went by their special route and Sid saw at once that the bricks had been tampered with. He put out a paw to stop Clappy.

"They've been moved," he whispered.

"What?"

"The bricks. We always leave them in the same place, but they're not like we left them. They've been moved." He slipped through the gap.

"Must be Bennett."

"Who else? We've got a problem. Looks like he's on to us."

They climbed down the sacks.

"He built this lot so he could spy on us." Clappy shook his head. "He might have seen Alf."

"Certain! Get the fruit quick. Batty'll know what to do."

They went back next door and carefully left the bricks as they had found them.

"He can't have seen much. It's only a narrow gap." They were discussing Sid's discovery.

"But he's spying on us, Sid. He'll have another look when he gets back tonight." Weston was worried.

"Then we'll be ready for him."

"Right, Totters!" Orse agreed. "If Bennett puts his eye to that gap again we'll give him a surprise – give him a squirt of something."

"Lemons," suggested Totters. "An eyeful of lemon juice

is painful – and we could use his own lemons."

"Or onions . . . they sting. We could mix them and get Alf to give him a squirt, like he did in the bath." Orse laughed. "Might make him fall off the sacks."

"And break his leg . . ."

They laughed, but Batty quietened them. He was thinking. "It's an idea and he deserves it, but it won't solve the problem. We've got to be ahead of him. What's that long word you know, Weston?"

"Psychological?"

"That's it – thinking – we've got to do some of that. We can make Bennett angry any day. It's simple because he's simple."

"He's daft."

"I know, but this time we've got to do it like Weston says. We'll surprise him all right, but we won't make him mad. We'll make him happy." He wiped his whiskers. "That's it. This time we'll make him believe what he sees." He pointed to the loose bricks. "He looks through there so we'll give him something to see."

"What, Batty?"

"I'm working it out, Totters, don't rush me. Sid, nip next door and put your eye right up close. Have a look through. Tell us what you see."

They waited until Sid shouted.

"Right, Sid. What can you see?"

"An armchair. I can see the top of it with the lace bit."

"Just what you'd expect to see in a place like this," said Totters, "an armchair in a junk store, that's normal."

Batty ignored the interruption. "Wait a bit, Sid, stay there. Weston, bring Alf over and sit him in his chair." He frowned as he worked it out. They needed to know exactly what Bennett might have seen. "OK, Sid, what can you see now?"

"A gorilla – a white gorilla – Alf."

"A what?"

"Sorry, Batty, it's an old man. I can see an old man with a white face."

"You're sure?"

"Well just his head. The gap's not very big. You can only see the top of him from here."

Batty looked grim. It was bad luck they had Alf's chair in exactly that position. He scratched one of his bald patches. Bennett could not be trusted. He must have seen Alf. He might even have seen him before he changed colour. It was a nasty thought. There was a reward out for the gorilla, and Bennett was greedy.

Batty had another scratch. It might just be possible to show Bennett that he could believe what he saw with his own eyes. It would be risky. They hardly had time – he looked at his watch – but they were ahead of Bennett by about two hours. If they started at once and hurried all the way they might be able to get back before him. He made up his mind. They had to take the risk.

Chapter Twenty

"Why couldn't we just get Oily Sludge and paint him white and tie him to the chair?" Totters was riding in the pram with the others.

"He wouldn't look right," said Sid, "and stop complaining . . . and wriggling. You're making it uncomfortable for all of us."

"It's Alf's fault, not mine. He's going too fast. He's bumping us all over the place."

"He's got to go fast. We're in a hurry. Keep still. We're in the main road. You're supposed to be the baby."

They were on their way to Kensington, where the museums are, and they were counting the minutes. For the operation to work they had to arrive at the museum just after closing time. Then, if they could get the job done in ten minutes, they would have time to get back to the arches before Bennett came from the market. It was going to be close.

"Turn left here, Alf." Weston pulled his ear. "Five minutes to closing time, Batty."

Alf rattled the pram along the pavement. He understood that something urgent was on, and was going as fast as he could.

"Three minutes . . . two . . . nearly there. That's it, Batty, that's the place." Weston pointed ahead. His navigation had been perfect. "The big building across the road."

"Well done. We're on time."

They crossed the road.

"Now go along by the railings and in the gate, but not in the front door, Alf. Go into the gardens and round the side . . . and along the path to the last bench. Wait here. It's safe. You can have a rest." Weston jumped down.

It was not an unusual sight in the museum garden. Alf sat gently rocking the pram like anyone else with a baby to look after. Batty stayed with him, but the others followed Sid through a basement window into the museum.

It was gloomy inside. In some places the light was completely blocked by cupboards or glass cases but Sid had a torch.

Weston stopped by a foot with long claws. He shuddered, but it was not what they wanted. He looked up the scaly leg. "Ostrich – I remember it," he whispered. "The one we want's a bit further on."

Orse gave them a fright when he bumped into a crocodile. It was stiff and propped against the wall, and it slipped slowly sideways until it crashed in a cloud of dust. It made him sneeze.

"Bless you . . ."

"Quiet, Totters!" Sid shone his torch. "Where is it, Weston?"

"It's this way."

They went on.

"Here somewhere, I think. It should be about here."

Sid halted them. He swept the beam slowly round. It was

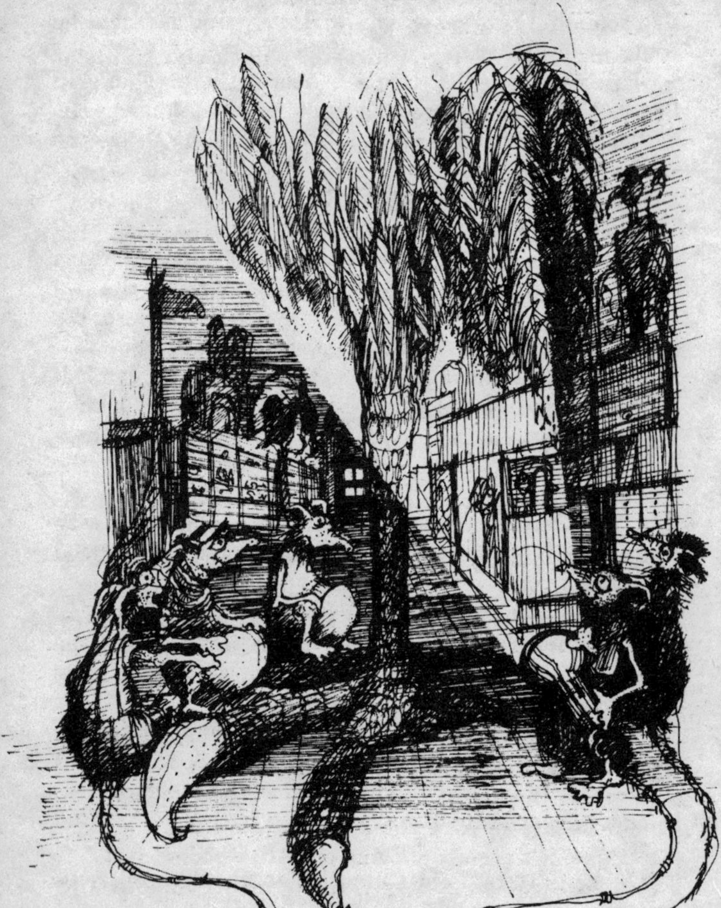

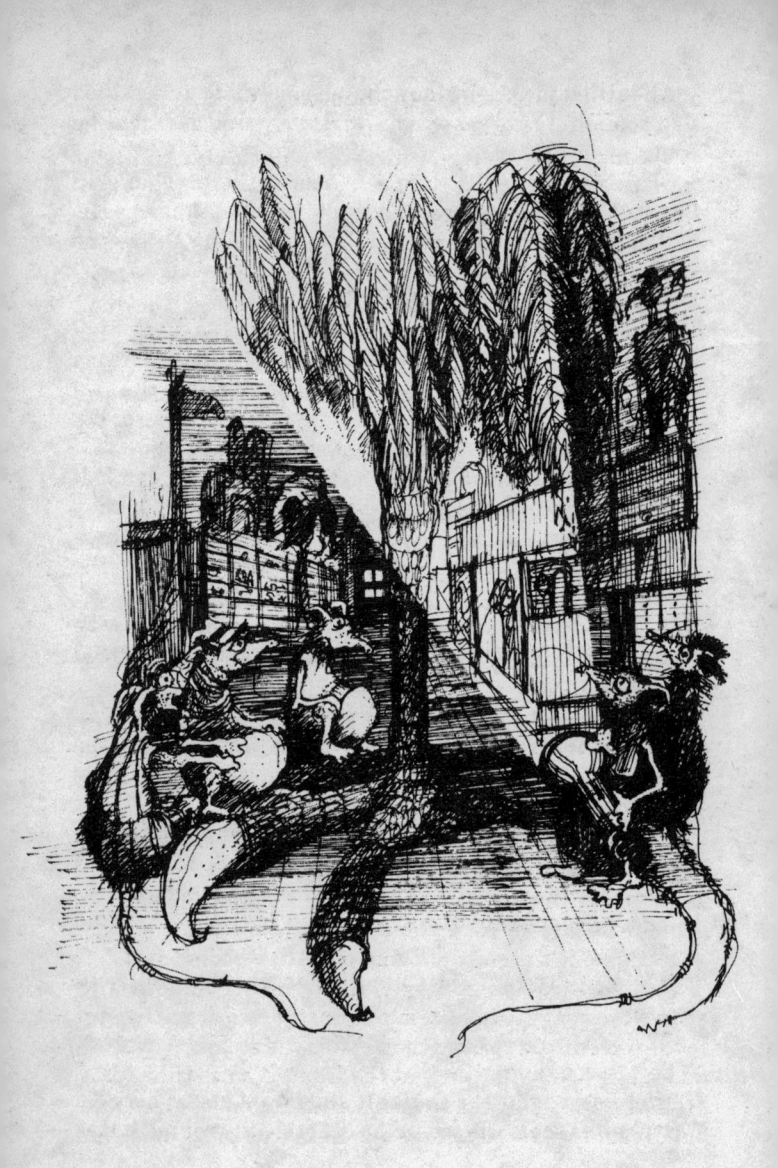

a bit frightening because the light kept picking out eyes which seemed to stare at them.

"That's it . . ." Weston whispered. "Back a bit, Sid, a bit more . . . there!"

Sid shone the beam up and down.

"It's him!" Weston was excited. It was even better than he remembered. "Like Batty said – just what we need."

"String!" Sid only had to give the order once. They had been well briefed. Orse had a coil of string over his shoulder. He jumped and began to climb.

"Round his neck twice and back down to us. Throw the end down."

It fell at Sid's feet. "Ready? Ready all of you?"

Orse jumped down.

"Right, with me . . . all together . . . pull . . ."

"Careful!" Weston was alarmed. "He might be fragile. Be gentle with him."

There was no time to be gentle. "Pull . . ." Sid urged. He took a deep breath. "Hard . . . harder . . . pull . . ."

They had to jump out of the way as the string suddenly went slack. There was a dull thud which echoed through the basement and might have given them away, but they had to chance it. They could not wait. Even before the dust settled they started dragging. It was heavy and awkward getting through some of the narrow spaces. They pulled and pushed together until they were back at the window. Batty was on the pram waiting for them.

"Got him?"

Sid nodded. "Anyone about, Batty? He's big."

"No one, it's all clear. Come on, Alf, we need you."

They had trouble getting it through the window. The arms were sticking out too much, one sideways and one up in the air. Alf had to bend them. Then the stomach was too fat and he had to flatten it at the front. It was still a tight fit. In the end he had to wrap his arms round its chest and pull. It scraped on the frame and lost some of its hair, but

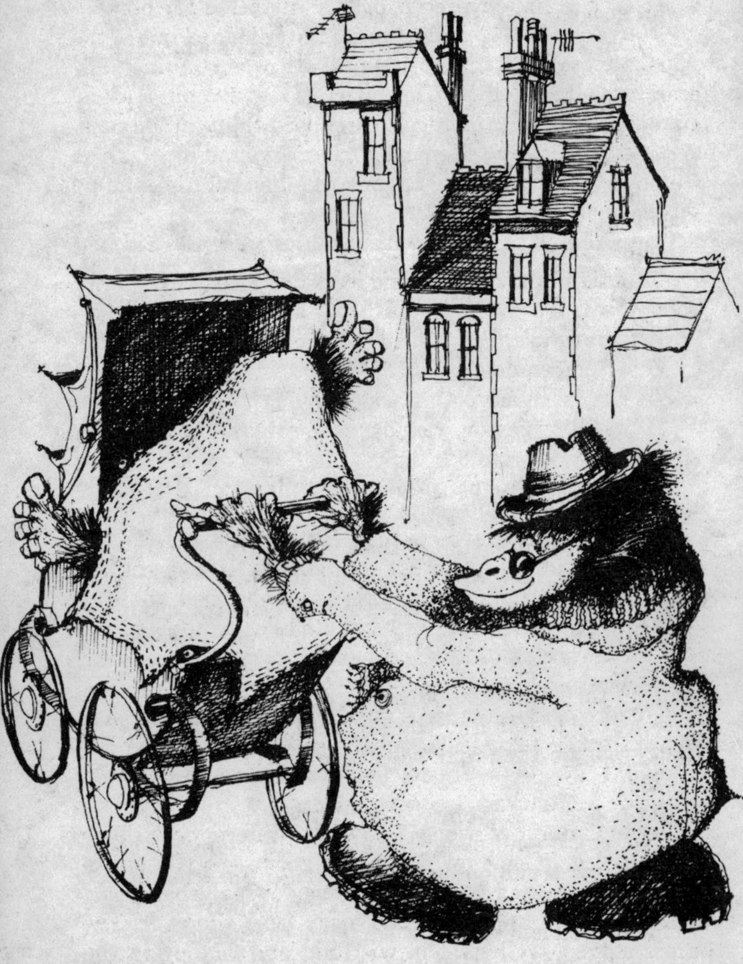

Alf grunted and pulled until he got it free. They squeezed it into the pram, covered it over and started for home.

"Well done, Sid . . . all of you." Batty leaned out of the scarf. He had to hang on because Alf was running. The pram was heavier but his arms were strong and he managed some high bounces. He caused chaos in the rush-hour traffic. "Silly old man!" Drivers wound down their windows and shouted, and shook their fists at him, and he waved back cheerfully.

They crossed the river with minutes to spare. Sid had gone on ahead, and when he met them with the news that Bennett was not back, Batty knew they had a chance.

Alf steered the pram through the door and climbed the barricade easily with the load tucked under one arm. He dropped it on the mattresses and Batty made signs for him to pick it up and put it in the armchair. Alf was not sure.

"Don't worry." Batty understood how he felt. He could see him frowning. "It's only temporary." He patted his hand. "We only want your chair for a little while."

The orang-utang which they had borrowed was the nearest thing they could get to a gorilla. It was stuffed, and after its treatment was looking a bit battered, but they went to work on it. They brushed its hair and dusted the eyes till they shone. It was an elderly orang-utang with lots of wrinkles but they powdered the hair to make it look even older. When they were finished it might easily have been mistaken for Alf. It had the same big jaw and flat nose, and the glass eyes set back behind the brow were bright. It was almost a good likeness.

"Perfect! Bennett won't know the difference." Batty was satisfied. "Come on, Alf, we've got to get you out of the way." Batty and Weston went back over the barricade with him and along the wharf away from the gate. The others stayed, well hidden, with Sid and Clappy in the armchair behind the orang-utang.

They were so quiet that they heard the barrow much

sooner than usual. They heard Bennett drag it in and put it away. He clattered around as though he wanted everyone to know he was back, and when he left he slammed the door hard. He walked to the gate whistling, something he never did.

They stayed still. Sid smiled as minutes later they heard him coming back. He tip-toed along the wharf and thought he had slipped into his store without being heard, but when he stood still for a moment they knew exactly where he was, and what he would do next. They counted his steps to the potatoes and heard the soft crunch as he started to climb. They knew when he was at the top. They could hear him breathing from the effort.

The old man was there – he looked again – still in the chair, staring up at him with eyes bright like glass, very much alive and moving.

Sid and Clappy judged it nicely. They were behind the orang-utang, one on each arm, pulling and pushing and rocking the body, and keeping themselves out of sight.

Bennett swallowed hard and looked again. He turned his head to get his eye closer, and blinked. He had been wrong. He could not believe his eye, and tried with the other one. It wasn't an old man at all. It was . . . it was . . . a gorilla . . . the gorilla . . . the escaped gorilla.

When he reached the ground beads of sweat were trickling down his face. He dared not make a sound. The gorilla! There was a reward. He had read about it. He wished he had looked before when he started missing a lot more fruit. He might have collected the reward already. He looked up at the gap. What a find! Just the other side of the wall! There was no mistaking the big chin and all the hair – a bit grey, but it was probably an old gorilla, and it was just like the pictures in the papers. They had been searching all over, and it was here all the time – next door. He had found it for them.

He wondered how much the reward was – a hundred

pounds, more like a thousand. Gorillas were worth a great deal of money. He rubbed the tips of his fingers together at the thought. They were rough like files, and the rats heard.

At last! Something good! Bennett forgot about the rats. He felt like singing as he let himself out. But he slipped away as silently as he had come, and had no idea that Sid and Orse, on Batty's orders, were a few paces behind him.

Chapter Twenty-One

At the zoo the Director was playing nervously with his bow-tie. It was very creased. The gorilla was still missing. He had concentrated the search in London where he was sure they would find him. The parks and open spaces had been thoroughly searched but they found nothing. He was beginning to think he might have been wrong.

He had hardly slept for a week and was very tired. He got up from his desk and looked out of the window. His hands were shaking. He rubbed his palms together, pinched his nose, scratched his ear – anything. He found it difficult to keep still. He turned to the wall-map and moved flags about.

He looked at his watch. He had spent another night alone in his office, and was about to start another day trying to keep control of the search. So many reports, from all sorts of people, he mumbled to himself, most people would not know a gorilla from – he was lost for a word and waved a hand in the air – from a grandfather. What time was it?

The telephone rang. It took him by surprise, and went

on ringing as he searched for it under the papers on his desk. Reports . . . sightings . . . more reports! He lifted the receiver.

"That the zoo?"

"The zoo? Yes, this is the zoo."

"You lost a gorilla."

"A what?"

"You lost a gorilla? It was in the papers." The voice was very rough. "The gorilla you lost. . ."

"What about it?" He fingered the reports.

"I know where it is."

Almost certainly another false alarm.

"Did you hear? I know where it is. I know where your gorilla is."

"What did you say?" The Director could not help yawning.

"You listening?" The voice became more urgent. "I know where he is. I've seen him – twice."

The Director tried counting the flags in the map.

"You still there?"

So many of them, "Yes."

"This gorilla, the one you lost – can you still hear me?"

"Yes, of course."

"What I want to know is – is there a reward?"

"For the gorilla?" He rubbed his eyes. He was waking up. "A reward for the gorilla?"

"That's right."

"Yes, yes . . . there is a reward."

"How much?"

The Director wrote down the first figure that came into his head. "A hundred pounds."

"Not enough!" The reply snapped back. "A gorilla's worth more than that."

It was true. The gorilla was worth very much more than a hundred pounds. He was worth thousands. "Two hundred."

"No!"

"All right. How much do you want?"

"A thousand – a thousand pounds in notes and he's yours. I know where he is. I can take you straight to him."

The Director had to make up his mind. "All right, a thousand, but he's got to be alive and well."

"He's alive and well. I saw him move." The caller seemed so certain that the Director had to be interested. "You know where he is?"

"That's what I said. I'll show you. But you'll have to hurry. Bring the money and come down here. Bennett's the name. Number four arch, Battersea wharf. You cross the river at Chelsea bridge, turn left opposite the park and come in through the iron gates. I'll be waiting for you, and don't forget to bring the money. You'll get your gorilla back."

Bennett slammed the telephone down so hard that Clappy, who was hanging under it in the call box, almost fell off. Sid was waiting for him when he followed Bennett out. "What did he say?"

"The zoo. He phoned the zoo." They slipped from cover to cover, keeping Bennett in sight.

"They'll be on their way then. You stay with him." Sid went on ahead. He had to get the news to Batty. He took a short cut through private property and reported to him.

"What I expected!" He was ready. "Get it cleared – all of it. Leave it like it used to be. Leave it all in a mess . . . nothing on the table . . . strip the bed. And you, Alf . . ." He pointed. "You get him outside."

Alf understood.

It was as though a hurricane had struck. It took seconds for them to create chaos. Batty took a last look round and followed the others out to the wharf where Alf was waiting with the orang-utang under his arm.

"Lose him, Alf." Batty pointed to the river. "Chuck him in."

Alf did not need telling twice. He swung the orangutang round his head – and let go. He laughed as it sailed through the air and splashed into the river but there was no time to wave goodbye.

"Run . . . they're on their way from the zoo. You've got to get out of sight again. Quick!"

When Bennett arrived he made sure he was alone. With a thousand pounds almost in his pocket he could not risk being seen by anyone or disturbing the gorilla hiding next door. As far as he was concerned the money was all his. He understood now. The gorilla had nothing to do with the rats. That was just a coincidence. Anyone intelligent knew that gorillas and rats would not get on together. The gorilla must have come alone – obviously the night the celery disappeared, when he escaped from the zoo.

Bennett slipped into his store. All he had to do was wait for the experts and the money. He made himself comfortable on a sack of potatoes. It was very quiet, no sound from next door – that was a good sign. The gorilla must be asleep still.

He hunched his shoulders. A thousand pounds! He could hardly believe his luck. He had been looking for rats and he had found a gorilla, a famous gorilla. Not many people do that. A thousand pounds – he closed his eyes – for finding a gorilla. He leaned back, relaxed and well pleased with himself.

He did not hear the arrival of the experts from the zoo. They parked away from the entrance to the wharf, and approached on foot, making sure they would not disturb the gorilla – if he was there.

The Director led. He was wide awake now and more hopeful. It was exactly as he had been saying all the time. Their gorilla would not be far away. He could have walked to Battersea from the zoo. He counted the arches from the gate.

It was a grey morning, not yet fully light but he could see enough. He made a sign to the others to stop, and tiptoed by himself to number four arch. The door was slightly open. He looked in with his eyes partly closed to adjust to the gloom. He dare not risk using a torch.

As he tried to make out details of the interior his spirits rose. He became aware of the smell, rich and fruity like the kitchens at the zoo. Fruit! It was exactly the sort of smell that would attract a hungry gorilla.

His eyes adjusted slowly – boxes, baskets, sacks and – he could hardly believe it. He wanted to be sure. The shape was right – hunched up and with no neck, fast asleep on a sack of potatoes. He stepped back silently.

"Net . . ." He mouthed the word, and nodded in answer to his keepers' unspoken question. It was their gorilla at last.

The keepers were ready – four of them. They were well-built, specially chosen for the job, and each of them held the corner of a heavy net. The Director put a finger to his lips, then made a series of signs, explaining what they had to do. They nodded and bunched behind him, checking their grip on the net.

It was the Director's moment at last. The waiting was over. He took a deep breath, held it for a second and threw himself against the door. As it burst open he stepped aside, pointing. If he had shouted 'CHARGE' it would not have seemed out of place. The net ballooned as the keepers ran by him, and came down square on target.

The rush was stopped by the sacks of potatoes, but not the keepers. They overlapped the sides of the net, twisted and turned it urgently as though they were wrapping an enormous parcel.

"Round again. . ."

"Over to me . . ."

They did not bother with names.

"More rope . . ."

"To me..."

"Tie it..."

"Tighter..."

They went on tying even after the net was secured. They threw the rope round and round the bundle until they were sure they had the gorilla safe.

Their captive was doing everything an escaped gorilla would do. He was kicking and throwing himself about, grunting and puffing. The bundle was not still for a second but they were ready for him. They had enough rope to hold him. There was no escape this time.

When they relaxed at last the heap on the floor was like a giant chrysalis struggling to be born. They stood at a safe distance and watched the bundle straining and kicking.

"Got him!" The Director sighed and approached with a torch. He was happy at last, but took care to keep away from the flailing bundle. "Splendid! Are the knots tight? He's strong, you know."

"He won't get away." The head-keeper spoke confidently.

At last, after all the waiting and the worry he had his gorilla back. The Director's problem was over, and he had been right all the time. He shone his torch on the bundle. "Gentlemen," he said proudly, "we've got our gorilla back at last." As he spoke he looked straight into Bennett's eyes.

Bennett was speechless with shock, and out of breath from struggling. He managed to grunt though he had used up most of his strength, and when he looked into the light his eyes blazed and he drummed on the floor with his boots.

The Director aimed the light more carefully. The gorilla was wide awake. This was the tricky bit. He would be angry, and an angry gorilla would have the strength of ten men. An angry gorilla – he ran the light along the bundle, and did not want to believe what he saw – boots! He was better educated than Bennett but at that moment was just as lost for words. He held the torch still. It could not be – boots and trousers! Instead of a gorilla in the net they had a human being, homo sapiens, an adult male, and he was clearly not pleased to be there.

The Director's moment of triumph did not last long. He did not want to look any more. He turned sadly away and walked to the door. He handed the torch to his head-keeper and made a weary sign for him to sort it out.

It took a long time.

Bennett was bruised and sore and seething. At first he refused to talk. When he was finally freed he rubbed his arms and wrists where the ropes had burned, and pointed to the marks. The keepers did their best to calm him.

Of course it was him. They managed to get him to talk at last. He had telephoned the zoo, and he did know where their gorilla was. He was in the arch next door – not this one, but he doubted after all the noise they had made whether he would still be there. And he was right. When the head-keeper climbed up to look through the gap he could see nothing unusual – only junk. There was certainly no sign of a gorilla.

"He was there. I saw him." Bennett insisted, but when they went next door they found nothing. He went with them. There might still be a chance of the reward. It was a mess next door, and although they had a good look there was no gorilla, nor was there any sign of one – no banana skins or bits of fruit. There was just furniture, mostly junk and rubbish, exactly what they expected. They came out to the wharf where the Director was waiting.

He shook his head. A gorilla would never choose such a place. It was not in character. They formed a group with Bennett in the middle so that the Director could explain to him. An escaped gorilla, he pointed out, would look for a place where he could make a nest. He was not like humans. He would not be interested in furniture and would certainly not know how to sit in a chair, as Mr. Bennett had described seeing him. The Director waved his arms in a gesture round the wharf. This was not the place to look for a gorilla. This was a place for people, a built-up place of bricks and hard materials, very uncomfortable for a gorilla. What he would look for would be a natural place with trees and bushes, somewhere with leaves or straw so that he could make a nest and cover himself.

Bennett sulked as he listened.

It was fascinating, the Director went on, how gorillas lived and the way their minds worked. You had to be an expert to understand them. That was why Mr. Bennett had been mistaken. It was not really his fault. He was a greengrocer. He could not be expected to know anything about animals or their habits, especially gorillas.

The explanation went on, and they were all listening so attentively that none of them took any notice of the noise coming from nearby. It was just a lorry being started for the day's work. They went on talking and stepped carefully out of its way as it ground past them in low gear.

The Sludge-Gulper went through the gate with a friendly honk and with a bucket clattering loosely at the back. As it passed the group none of them gave the driver a second look. They were absorbed in the lecture on gorillas, and none of them noticed his white hair or dark glasses, nor that the was wearing a cap very much like the keepers.

Nor could any of them anticipate that when the Director got away from the wharf and from Mr. Bennett later in the morning and went back to his desk he would find a report of another sighting. A gorilla had been seen swimming across the Thames at Greenwich.

He got another report later of a gorilla seen at Gravesend, lower down river, heading out to sea.

He had no faith in the reports – gorillas were not natural swimmers. What he was never to know was that the sawdust in the stuffed orang-utang started to swell when it got wet. It swelled so much that the animal burst its skin and sank somewhere down river from Tilbury. It was a peaceful end for a fine old beast who had once roamed free through happier places than the basement of a London museum.

* * *

PS   Alf is still free. If you happen to see him, an old man in a hat – it might be any sort of hat now – and a scarf, and wearing dark glasses, with a shopping bag or bulging pockets; if you spot him with his white hair sticking out of the sides of his hat, alone or in a crowd; or if you see him resting – perhaps on a park bench, in your town or at the seaside, don't give him away. Look out for him wherever you might be. And if you see him – whatever you do, don't say anything. Just smile to yourself and keep our secret. It will make Alf and us very happy if you do that.

signed

Weston
(for Batty)

PPS   And look out for Oily Sludge. He's a nasty piece of work.

You can see more Magnet books
on the following pages

The Duck Street Gang

DENIS MARRAY

Class 2D are a force to be reckoned with, as Mr. Wordsworth, the student teacher at Duck Street School, soon discovers. Ordinary school events turn rapidly into nightmares, there was the extraordinary affair of the hand grenades, and their revolutionary version of the school nativity play . . .

Runner-up for the Guardian Award

'Hilarious'   THE GUARDIAN

'Rip-roaring St Trinian's type stuff'   THE STANDARD

The Duck Street Gang Returns

DENIS MARRAY

Class 2D are back again in full force after the summer holidays. The Autumn term begins with The Great Conker Expedition . . . moving on to making gas-masks for pigeons and the fateful painting competition. But the headmaster's anxiety reaches fever-pitch when a TV company wish to use the infamous school for a children's programme . . .

Swings and Roundabouts

JEAN URE

Jason is all set to make his showbiz debut on TV, fame and fortune seem to be within his grasp and then the part goes to someone else. Dejected and ridiculed Jason learns a hard lesson. But the outcome of it all is most surprising . . . it's all swings and roundabouts . . .

Witness

DAVID JOHNSTONE

Witness to a brutal killing, Red is soon pursued by the evil Jacob Slattery, the murderer himself. Slattery's one aim is to silence Red and keep his foul crime a secret. Fleeing to London, Red seeks refuge in the violent, teeming streets. But the orphan has more enemies than friends . . .

Full of atmosphere and memorable characters, this is a tense and compelling thriller.

The Snow Spider

JENNY NIMMO

'Time to find out if you are a magician!' said Gwyn's grandmother, as she gave him five strange birthday gifts. What could they mean? The piece of seaweed, the yellow scarf, the tin whistle, the twisted metal brooch and the small broken horse? Gwyn gave the brooch to the wind and, in return, there came a tiny silver spider, Arianwen. The snow spider . . .

A rich and enthralling story of love, friendship and magic.

Grand Prix Winner of the Smarties Prize for Children's Books

'A heart-warming fantasy' THE GUARDIAN